A god-touched vigilante
With a desperate plan
Challenges a devoted order

ROGUE MAGE

10TH ANNIVERSARY EDITION

SAGA OF THE GOD-TOUCHED MAGE
BOOK THREE

RON COLLINS

SKYFOX
PUBLISHING
Fantasy

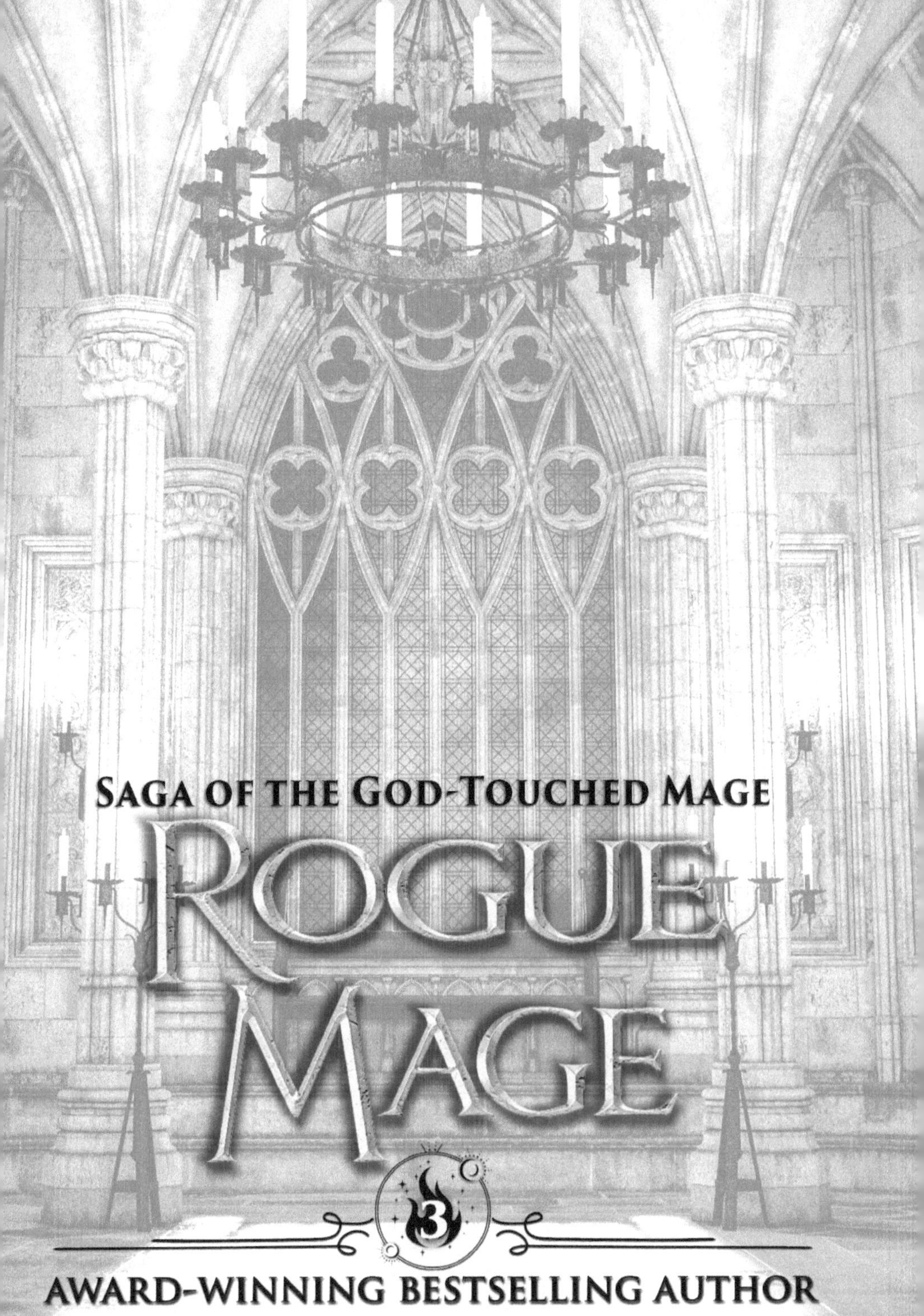

Saga of the God-Touched Mage
ROGUE MAGE
3
AWARD-WINNING BESTSELLING AUTHOR
RON COLLINS

The Saga of the God-Touched Mage
10th Anniversary Edition
includes

Apprentice Mage
Rogue Mage
Champion Mage
God Mage

FOREWORD: SATISFACTION

I recently posted someplace that Devo's version of the Rolling Stones' "Satisfaction" was the greatest cover of all time.

I stand by that.

I admit that I'm not a big fan of covers, though. I tend to weigh the original creator's version the highest of all, then gear down from there. Neil Young's "Helpless" is god-like. K.D. Lang's is also amazing (because literally everything K.D. Lang does is amazing), but it's amazing cosplay.

Which, is, of course, fantastic of itself.

Great cosplay is massive fun.

I do like a lot of covers, but I generally like them when they do something different with them. Like Devo did with "Satisfaction." Or Cat Power, for that matter, who completely changed the point of the song.

Why, you might ask, however, am I talking about an old rock group's old song right now? Isn't this supposed to be a foreword to the tenth anniversary of *Saga of the God-touched Mage?* Where's the conversation about Garrick, and Darien, and ... Well. It's like this.

I'm thinking about "Satisfaction" because in working through the pages that comprise this book, it struck me that the song's title isn't just "Satisfaction." It's "(I Can't Get No) Satisfaction." And in a very real sense, that's where we find Garrick now. The previous volume sees him win the day but come, in process, to the understanding that it's not all over now--that Roseanne Roseannadanna (to bring in another old pop culture reference) was right when she said, "It's always something."

That's something I like about a lot of great stories.

Even when the character wins, they lose. Or, as good story structure demands, things get worse. Steadily and with certainty. It's like the main character is on a forever-losing streak, right? Until the end, when … well, that's jumping ahead of myself now, isn't it?

I have a tendency to do that, too.

In *Rogue Mage* we're looking at the fallout that comes about as Garrick deals with the ramifications of his "victory" and gains maybe an even deeper idea of what life is about.

That's something that happens in real life, too, right?

We learn things when things go wrong--or when things go right, but now you've got something else to deal with. The world is big, isn't it? Sometimes we don't understand the game we're playing until something happens and reality punches us right in the nose.

Life goes on, though, and everything we do just builds and builds to the point that, eventually, things come together in ways that teach us something—or at least make us feel wise. The scars we build up over a lifetime are yardsticks, of a sort. They each define a piece of our quests for whatever we determine might be satisfaction. The accumulation of those scars can be frustrating, painful, and annoying. The path of getting through them can certainly feel like the phrase "I can't get no" relates directly to us.

We have to go through them, though.

That is life, right?

The alternative is certainly not exciting.

On that cheery note, I'll say this about how I felt writing this part of the saga—I think these are the struggles that wind up defining him, his reactions to them, anyway. Just like it is our reactions to the problems that confront us during the stories of our lifetimes that define us.

I should also say that of the four new volumes that have sprung from the original eight, I found this one to be the most challenging, and most delightful. This is because the original two books the *Champion Mage* is comprised of were, to be honest, the tiniest bit of a sprawling mess. The storylines are all over the place. When I split the original narratives into eight pieces, it was these two books that taxed readers the most, asking them to hold pieces of the stories together across the volumes.

They worked as they were, but I have been struck with how much happier I am now that the two are together and able to breathe as one.

I guess this means the Stones were wrong.

It turns out that I can, indeed, get satisfaction.

Ron Collins
Las Vegas — 2025

For Tim, Mike, Jackie, and Ken. And of course, for Lisa.

MAP OF ADRUIN

PROLOGUE

Braxidane felt his siblings' presence before he saw them. He had been expecting them, so he watched from his node as Agar and Hezarin flowed through the gray space of connectivity between the thousand worlds.

"Sister!" he said as they entered. "Brother! How fine it is to sense you."

"Give us our mages back," Agar replied. His voice was a cold pulse in the media of Existence.

"What do you mean?"

"You know exactly why we are here," Hezarin replied in a tone that crackled with the odor of acid on metal. She was like that, Braxidane thought, always oozing exaggerated responses.

Braxidane pulled himself into a tight shape that might have been a sphere if shape had meaning here.

She was right, of course.

He did know exactly why they were here.

His siblings had been fighting over Adruin, a plane of barely moderate import, if that. Each was trying to strengthen their presence by controlling more of the plane's flow. Agar had endowed his

Lectodinian mage with his form of draining magic, and Hezarin had given her Koradictine caster a burning energy full of fire and consumption. Their two champions had been full-bodied mages of great experience before receiving their god-touch, and were nearly invincible afterward. Yet somehow Garrick—Braxidane's own champion, a mage barely past his apprenticeship—had managed to snare them in a loop of magic that would, unless Braxidane stepped in, last for eternity.

He shivered with delight. It served his siblings right.

"Don't lay blame on me, sister," he said. "Linking Parathay and Jormar was Garrick's doing."

"Semantics, *brother*," Hezarin responded. "Garrick's magic carries your touch."

"Certainly."

"So his work *is* your work," Agar said.

"Come, now. None of us controls every action of any of the mages we touch."

"We want our champions back," Hezarin said coolly.

"Actions and consequences," Braxidane said. "Both of you should have considered that before you broke the agreement."

"It's a meaningless plane," Agar replied.

Braxidane flooded his essence with a hint of blue-green sweetness that said Agar's defense missed the entire point.

"We agreed," he said. "That none of us would disturb another existence without everyone's acceptance."

"It's an agreement rarely followed."

"I have followed it," Braxidane said, flashing self-righteousness with purposeful intent.

Agar snorted. "Don't make me laugh."

"Enough!" Hezarin said. Her emotions flashed blue, and a curtain of gold filament floated around her. "Give us back our mages, or we'll take every plane you control."

"Dear sister Hezarin," Braxidane said. "You're always good for an ultimatum. Do any of them ever work?"

"Are you asking for magewar on Adruin?" she said.

"Do I detect hypocrisy, dear Hezarin? You're usually so adamant about saving lives and protecting your constituency."

Hezarin spewed orange sparks.

Agar moved to exist between them.

"Come, Braxidane," he said. "If we're to come to resolutions on this, we'll all have to get past our jealousies."

"I don't see that we have any resolution to come to, brother Agar. My champion's work is done. There is no value in adjusting it."

Hezarin could contain herself no further, then. She lashed out at him, her tendrils looping around Agar's barrier so quickly he could barely constrain her.

Braxidane raised his defenses.

"That's enough," he said. "You come into my node, demanding I take action for something I'm not responsible for. You insult me with accusations. And now you attack me physically. If you can't behave, then get out of my node."

He twisted his thoughts and pushed against her.

"You'll regret this," she wailed as she allowed herself to be swept away.

Braxidane waited silently.

His brother turned even colder than usual.

"I think that was a mistake," Agar said with his usual reserved calm.

"Actions and consequences," Braxidane replied. "I'll take my chances."

Under a blood-red sunset, Garrick rode hard atop a lathering charger. Fall was soon to give to winter. The air chilled his cheeks and seared his lungs. Hooves thundered against the hard ground of open plain as he bolted across the horizon, determination etched on his face. It was a face growing older than his years, now, a face that had seen more death and more pain than any should. The wind pulled tears from the corners of his eyes.

Hunger flared inside him.

That hunger was a pain, a gnawing flare that bloomed and raged. It was sacrifice and it was horror. It was subservience. He pushed himself harder, urging the horse to race faster, using pure speed and exhilaration to rid himself of the depths of this ache.

Tall grass rolled past in brittle waves, its color the browns and yellows of a dead fall. The animal's muscles rolled beneath him, rhythmic and fluid, forelegs reaching, hind legs driving. Garrick pressed into the stride, driving with all his strength. The muscles of his shoulders and legs burned so boldly they blunted the darkness that had grown within him. The beast snorted a complaint, but Garrick responded by driving the animal harder.

Finally, they crested a hill and came to the edge of the forest. Mercifully, Garrick brought the horse up.

Its breath billowed with misty plumes in the evening air. Its coat was lathered to a sheen.

A hawk soared in the sky.

"It's not going to work, you know?"

Garrick turned to his left. A tall gray heron with deep black eyes stood beside a large rock that protruded from the hillside. It was his mage superior, the planewalker who was the source of this wicked curse he carried.

"Braxidane," he said. "I was wondering when I would see you again."

The heron took a step forward with a motion that was all knee. "You shouldn't fight your nature," it said.

"I fight only what makes sense to fight."

"And it makes sense to fight your true powers?"

"They kill randomly."

"Randomly?"

Garrick said nothing.

Braxidane dipped his heron head.

"There is nothing random about your powers, Garrick—just as there is nothing random about your responsibilities."

Braxidane was talking about the Freeborn, Garrick knew. The planewalker wanted to use him to control the new Torean House, but Garrick had no interest in such leadership. He had even less desire to give Braxidane any such boon.

"I never asked for that responsibility."

"Nor does a coyote ask for his."

"I am not an animal."

"That's right, Garrick. Animals do not fight their destiny."

Garrick scoffed and turned away. "You make a good jest, Braxidane. But I'm more like a disease than an animal. What destiny does a disease have?"

"You are full of opinions, Garrick. So, let me ask you for another.

Just what should a man do when his brothers need him for a task that he has no stomach for?"

Garrick kept his gaze on the horizon. The ride had calmed his hunger, but hollowness still churned within him. He would need to feed again soon. The idea made him shudder. He thought then of the battle at God's Tower, and the warriors who had died there.

And he thought of Sunathri.

He wheeled to face his superior. "A proper leader doesn't destroy—"

The heron was gone.

Garrick gritted his teeth and reveled in the pain that sharp air brought to his lungs.

He had been in the wild for weeks now, hunting for Lectodinians, finding them one-by-one, and taking his vengeance upon each. Perhaps it was not as pretty as one might want, but it was something. And it kept the others safe. The Freeborn were in better hands with Darien and Reynard. He wasn't going to put the men and women of the Torean House in that kind of danger again.

He turned the horse toward his camp.

Will would have dinner prepared, and it was late enough that the boy would be worried.

Tomorrow Garrick had another mage to destroy.

His hunger stirred at the thought.

Yes.

Tomorrow.

He would hunt again tomorrow.

TWO

Wintertime brought raging storms and cold tides that crashed like battering rams against the volcanic cliffs of de'Mayer Island. It was a harsh place, rocky and wind-whipped, isolated. It was due to this isolation that its namesake, the famous general Corid de'Mayer, had been shackled here and left to fend for himself in the island's deepest catacombs. It was also due to this isolation that the Koradictine order of mages had made it their stronghold.

Deep in the workings of Areguard, the ancient fortress built into the rock overlooking the westernmost shoreline, Ettril Dor-Entfar, Lord Superior of that Koradictine order, stood before a water-filled decanter and an empty brazier at the center of his private chamber. A relief map of Adruin spanned the far wall and told a story that was not to his liking. The order's losses at God's Tower had been extreme, and word of their weakness had triggered uprisings across the whole of their holdings. They had never been strong in the eastern half of the plane, but they had lost Mordwood in the northwest, and Daggertooth to the south. They had been run out of Whitestone and the entirety of the Wildlands.

Now, even Badwall Canyon appeared to be shaken.

At least de'Mayer Island was still theirs. For now.

He pursed his lips. He had to rally his forces. The Koradictine order had to make a statement before they lost too much.

Ettril spoke magic and strolled carefully around the decanter, choosing the right moment to slowly spill its water into the basin. Leverage points passed energy from Talin, the plane of magic, through his link. The water boiled with the smell of curdled blood. More water flowed into a thin layer at the bottom of the basin, cooling it, then shimmering with the beginnings of an image. Ettril lifted the spell further, pulling detail to the surface until it became a woman's rounded face.

It was Iona, the ranking mage of Badwall Canyon.

Her wiry hair was unkempt and her lips were thick and red. She seemed to be out of breath.

"Your timing is impeccable," she said. "The Lectodinians are here, and they are here in force. They've convinced the townspeople to revolt. The situation is dire."

"It is good to see you, too, Iona," Ettril replied.

"I don't have time for this, Superior."

"I'll be brief, then. Badwall Canyon cannot fall. I need you to lead a counter-attack. You must crush any and all resistance."

Iona laughed.

"You *are* an old fool, Ettril."

"Be careful how you address me. I'll not take insolence lightly."

A pounding came from behind her, the sound of footsteps in an outside corridor. Iona glanced nervously over her shoulder.

"The order is dead, Superior. It may not appear that way sitting in the comfort of your island. But even if I wanted to execute your orders, there is no one left here to command."

"You are a coward!"

"No, Superior. I'm just a mage trying to stay alive."

The pounding came from the door again, this time accompanied by shouting voices that Ettril couldn't make out.

"And right now," Iona said, "I'm a mage who has to get out of town before its citizens string me up. News travels, Superior. They know we're weak, and they're making us pay for our boldness this past spring."

"I demand you stand and fight."

"Goodbye, Ettril."

"I'll execute you myself if I have to."

"Then I'll be seeing you soon. But right now, I'm leaving before the sheriff breaks the door down."

Iona stood, and the basin clouded.

Ettril sat back with acid flaring in his stomach. She was fleeing Badwall. Casius was holding Farvane, but not as a Koradictine stronghold. Jormar, the Koradictine god-touched, was lost in God's Tower, somehow defeated by the Torean champion. No Koradictine leader had faced such upheaval in the centuries since Koradic himself had founded the order.

"Bosic!" he called to his assistant.

Rustling came from the hallway, and the door whispered open.

"Yes, sir?"

"Come here," Ettril said with a calmness that belied his emotions.

Bosic shut the door behind him, and scuttled in with a shambling limp caused by his club foot. His robe was Koradictine red with a dark blue collar turned up. Its sleeves hung loosely at his wrists.

"What can I get you, Superior?"

"I need every high mage on the island here tomorrow morning as the sun rises."

"Yes, sir. Anything else?"

Ettril thought. "No."

"It will be done, sir."

Then Bosic went away quietly.

That was more like it, Ettril thought. A rapid response to a direct command. And it would be done, too. Bosic had been his apprentice since he was a child. He would never, of course, be a high mage.

Some things just weren't meant to be. But Bosic never stopped trying, and he knew his place—both traits that were sorely lacking in many these days.

Ettril stood and faced his library.

He was getting old. His back ached, and a pop came from one knee. That didn't matter, though. He was still strong enough to control the order, and the first rule of control was to make sure no one got the wrong message.

It was time to make a statement.

And over his lifetime he had found that nothing commands obedience like the sight of a dead body.

Garrick crouched in the hallway.

He felt the Lectodinian's presence on the other side of the door. It was Tevaran Kigg, a powerful mage who was now in the middle of casting an intricate spell forged with energy from the plane of magic. Kigg had been among those who had joined the raid on his superior's manor so many months prior. It was time to exact his revenge.

Garrick's hunger reached out and touched the mage's life force. It was raw and bold, firmly connected to the man's body. He felt the mage's connection to the plane of magic in ways that were deep and disturbing. He didn't know whether to be embarrassed of himself for having such an intimate contact, or angry at himself for the fact that he had grown to enjoy it so greatly. Garrick could feel, for example, how every scrap of the Lectodinian's attention was consumed in his spell work, and that now was exactly the time to strike.

One sharp kick broke down the door.

He cast raw magic about the room as he drew his blade.

"Wha—" Kigg said. "What are you doing?"

"Avenging a wrong," Garrick growled as he swung.

The blade became red and blood–gored.

The mage's life force peeled off its body, tasting sweet and powerful. Garrick breathed it in like something physical, like blood, or like a heart beating inside a man's chest, as natural as an arm or a leg, as essential as breathing itself. He shuddered as he fought its panicked dance, and gasped as the life force struggled against the pull of his god–touched gravity. It was like a fish fighting on the line, a steady string of panicked pulls that eventually faded to dead weight.

When he was finished, Garrick left the mage's room as he had found it. He wanted nothing of this man beyond what he had now, and there were still horses to release.

Garrick completed those chores, then left the manor.

The mage's life force warmed him as he picked his way down the rocky outcropping to reclaim his mount. Two more Lectodinians remained on the list of those who had raided Alistair. When he was done with them, he would go west to hunt Koradictines. If his planning was adequate and he spaced them out properly, his tour could keep his hunger fed throughout the winter.

Garrick set his jaw and began to ride.

Will—who was perhaps twelve years old but was maturing rapidly—would be waiting. Garrick wasn't looking forward to the boy's wide-eyed stare or the questions it would bring.

Will had joined him with great enthusiasm, and Garrick had taken the boy along because he felt something about him that was hard to explain—a kinship or a connection, like Will was a brother of some kind. And for his part, Will seemed to think similarly. The boy understood Garrick, he *listened* like no one else did. The boy instinctively knew that Garrick's magic was different from others, and seemed to sense when it was best to stay away from him and when it was safe to be nearby.

And, of course, Will had saved his life.

Convincing him to stay behind as Garrick hunted was getting harder. But he remembered what it was like to be Will's age. He knew exactly how hard it was to take care of yourself, better yet someone else. Will shouldn't have to deal with that, and Garrick would do what it took to keep him safe.

WHEN GARRICK RETURNED TO CAMP, however, the boy was nowhere to be found.

Will's horse was still tied to a tree, and their fire pit still gave off thin wisps of smoke. The bedrolls had been prepared but were not yet loaded onto the animals.

Hackles raised along the nape of Garrick's neck.

"Will?" he said in a low voice.

He felt the presence of two people sitting behind a slab of shale that jutted from the ground nearby. He pulled his sword silently and reached for his link. He had been an idiot to leave Will alone, a fool to think the Lectodinians would take the swath of destruction he was cutting through their ranks sitting down.

He brought magefire to his fingertips and he turned the corner.

A mage *was* sitting on the rock beside Will, but he was not clad in Lectodinian blue or Koradictine red. This man was tall and thin, and dressed in black trousers. A travel cape, also black, was pulled over his green tunic.

"Garrick!" Will said, standing up.

Garrick gritted his teeth as he calmed himself. His magic had its head, and it was everything he could do to pull it back. He gazed at the young man standing beside Will.

"The Freeborn were to leave me be," Garrick said.

"Don't worry about Jawsie," Will said. "He's got a message for you."

"Jawsie?" Garrick replied, still holding his blade before him. "I don't recognize you."

"My name is Jaw Millerson," the mage said, holding out a hand. "I'm new in the Torean House."

Garrick finally sheathed his blade.

"A message?"

"Indeed, Lord," the mage said. "Two messages, actually."

"Go on."

"The first is that Superior J'ravi needs your voice. The house is struggling over several key points."

Garrick winced.

In a politically deft step that was made to draw the Freeborn together, his friend Darien—Lord of the Freeborn despite being a man without magic—had appointed Garrick to his board of consultants. Garrick promised to support his friend, but he had no interest in sitting at a table when there were Lectodinians left to hunt.

"And the second message?"

"Commander J'ravi wishes you to know that his father, Commander of the Dorfort guard, is not well, sir."

Garrick sighed.

Will, too, seemed to deflate. Darien's father had kept Will at the manor during the battle at God's Tower, and the boy had grown close to the commander.

"Is he going to be all right?" Will said.

"The physician cannot say, sir. But there are rumors that Commander J'ravi may be seeing his last."

Garrick's heart dropped further. If Darien were to lose his father now it would be a great blow, and one that would hit double–hard with the stress of keeping a house of mages together.

"Well, Will," he said. "It appears we're going to spend some time in a city after all."

Will, who had been enjoying their trek through the wooded countryside, gave an empty grin. "All right," he said. "If nothing else it'll be nice to have Imelda and Daventry's cooking for a while."

FOUR

"Do I have your full attention?" Ettril said.

Four mages nodded, each glancing at Iona's body, which was tacked to the wall with iron spikes. Ettril sat at a low table that held a single sheet of paper and a quill on its polished surface.

The four mages were Quin Sar, a sharp, experienced wizard who had been in the order since he was a boy, Fil, a legacy mage from a line in good stead, Hirl-enat, an elder—passed over again and again for his final trigger, but who spent his days watching the goings on within the order like an ancient buzzard, cackling with glee at the occasional carcass but content to wait until others had finished before feeding on them himself—and then Neuma, a young woman of obvious ambition who had been climbing the ranks swiftly— perhaps too swiftly, Ettril thought.

They were in a chamber under de'Mayer Island, a room large enough to hold three times as many sorcerers. Blood–tinted mage-light provided illumination. The mages sat, wrapping robes over their shoulders to ward against the unremitting chill.

"We are now the core of the order," Ettril said.

"Do we have enough mages left to even be an order?" Neuma asked.

"There she goes again," said Hirl-enat.

"What's that supposed to mean, old man?" Neuma snapped.

"It means you've been able to step over other mages by exposing their weaknesses," Hirl-enat said in a crusty voice, his bushy brow twisting like a wooly worm. "But I think you're making a mistake trifling with the superior. Unless, of course," he glanced at the young woman, "you intend to *be* the superior?"

"I would never—"

"That's enough," Ettril said. "We have an order until I no longer draw breath. Have no mistake about that."

The mages quieted.

Neuma sat in a silent huff, and Hirl-enat gave a satisfied snuffle. Fil merely shifted about nervously.

Quin Sar, however, stared with distracted indifference. Ettril knew how dangerous it was to mistake Quin Sar's expression, though. The mage had not come by his powers randomly. Quin Sar saw and heard all, and he possessed a sadistic streak that provided him with intuitively divine and considerably effective ways to expose weaknesses.

Ettril scanned the four of them, his hand resting on the ivory ball at the end of his staff.

"Neuma's question is fairly made, though," Ettril said. "The Koradictine order is suffering the greatest peril of its long history, and it's up to us to take action now."

"So, what do we do?" Neuma asked.

Ettril twisted his hand over the ivory orb. A translucent map appeared in the air before him, de'Mayer Island far to the west, the mainland looming eastward, the Daggertooth mountains to the north. Badwall Canyon sat on the mainland's western coast. Dorfort commanded the central and southeastern plains. The wildlands of Whitestone, Warville, and Crystal Island lay to the far south.

"The Lectodinians were not damaged at God's Tower as gravely as we were," Ettril said.

A rune symbolized the solitary mountain where the orders had recently clashed. Captain el'Mor was supposedly trapped there, locked, if rumors were true, in a loop of magic with the Lectodinian god–touched mage.

"They have a stronghold somewhere here, in the Vapor Peaks."

An area to the north glowed with green enhancements.

"Where do we still have people?" Quin Sar said, his voice smooth as water over worn stone.

"Scattered," Neuma replied self–assuredly. "Our communications have broken down, and we don't have a power base we can count on."

"Neuma," Ettril said, fighting the urge to strangle her.

Hirl-enat's accusation of Neuma's ambition had a strong vein of truth to it—she *was* ambitious, and the order was in chaos. It would not be beyond her to seize such an opportunity. *I should kill her now*, he thought. But he needed her for what would come next, and if he let his emotions get the best of him now, his order would be done.

Neuma sat upright under Ettril's questioning gaze. "Did you not want the truth, Lord Superior?"

"I *see* the truth," Ettril said, making his voice sharp as a stiletto and his gaze sharper still. "Never doubt that."

The young mage sat quietly, her mouth firmly shut but her gaze placed just as firmly on Ettril's.

"After the fiasco at God's Tower," Ettril said, turning briskly back to the map, "our people *are* scattered. Our first task will be to gather them up again."

Quin Sar spoke. "They won't follow unless we have something to give them."

"What do you mean?" Ettril asked, knowing he could count on Quin Sar to lead the conversation where it needed to go.

"If our mages trusted our viability, they would be here already."

"You're right, of course," Ettril responded. "We need to show them we are still powerful, we need to show them we can create a dominant order."

"Yes," Quin Sar said. "They need to know we can survive."

Ettril stifled a knowing grin. Quin Sar, for all his idiosyncrasies, was a man who had come far and would go further. Unlike Neuma, he had opened the door for his superior to step through first.

"And for that we need to rid the plane of the one force who can truly stand in our way," Ettril said, pausing for effect. "We know now that Garrick, the Torean god–touched mage, has returned to Dorfort. I will travel there, and I will bring back his head."

"I think that's a mistake," Neuma said.

"Do you?" Ettril said, stepping precisely to cast a dark shadow over the younger mage. "Do you think I am too old to suffer such a trip? Or maybe too far removed from the arts to be able to cast against the god–touched? Do you take me for feeble?"

"No, Superior," Neuma replied, her gaze suddenly unable to meet Ettril's. "I did not say that."

"Then I suggest you speak clearly."

"I was in the east before the mage war," Neuma said. "I chased Garrick across the plane, so I know a bit about him. I've seen him slip away from powerful mages. I've seen him kill. I'm not suggesting he would best you, Lord Superior, but I think direct confrontation in Dorfort is a losing proposition."

"And you have a better suggestion."

Neuma hesitated.

"Perhaps it's not a better suggestion. But I have an alternative you might want to consider."

Ettril nodded, smirking inside. The young woman could learn. That was good. He straightened.

"Then let me hear it."

"Among the reasons Garrick was able to defeat our god–touched mage, as well as the Lectodinian's, was that he chose the battle-ground. He selected a place where he could separate our mages."

Ettril remained stoic.

Quin Sar nodded.

"As powerful as you are, Superior, we should not lose the fact that Garrick is god–touched and should not be trifled with. I think we need to dictate the events of your meeting."

"How do you propose we do that?" Quin Sar asked before Ettril was forced to.

"Garrick has a weakness," Neuma said. "We should use it to bring him to a place of our choosing, and at a time of our convenience."

All eyes were definitely now on Neuma.

Warming to the attention, the young mage spoke of her time in Caledena, and her experiences with Garrick. When she was finished, Ettril Dor-Entfar, Lord Superior of the Koradictine order, had a plan that would make the statement he so desperately wanted to make and a plan that would make Garrick come to him.

As they broke their session, Ettril let his gaze fall over Neuma. He had not gotten to his position without sensing the depths of his membership, and his gaze took in a woman of action, a woman of intellect, and a woman of political acumen.

Not at all, he thought, like Iona.

He realized, now more than ever, that Neuma was a woman to be watched.

FIVE

Garrick let loose the arrow, and the bow gave a satisfying twang. The bolt flew with a wobble, burying itself into the farthest edge of a target thirty paces away.

"Hoping you can best your apprentice, Garrick?"

He grumbled and turned to face Reynard. They'd been in Dorfort less than a week, and already he was feeling restless.

"Will is not yet my apprentice. I am not teaching him any magic."

Reynard shrugged. "Either way, the boy's still a better shot than you'll ever be."

Garrick rested his hand on the tip of his longbow.

He wore a black jerkin that was slightly too large for him, and breeches tucked into boots that came to mid-calf. Sweat glistened from his brow and brought him a chill despite the unseasonable midday heat. A pair of guardsmen fought a practice bout at the edge of earshot, grim and silent during their skirmishes, but jesting loudly between. Garrick was fighting a headache due to a lack of sleep, and the effort he expended fighting the power inside him did nothing to help.

"I came out here to get away from the meetings and the arguments," Garrick said. "What did you come here for? As if I can't guess?"

Reynard and Garrick comprised Darien's Council of Sorcery, ostensibly set to make policy for how magic would be developed and shared among members of the new Torean House. But Darien and Reynard were scuffling over every nuance of how the Freeborn should be run, both thinking their way was proper and neither willing to give any space for nuance.

"We need to discuss your friend," Reynard said.

"There is nothing to discuss."

"The man knows nothing about magic."

"Darien is doing what he thinks is best."

"He is shackling the Torean House."

Garrick glanced forlornly at the target, and pushed against the long bow, feeling its bend against his palm.

"The mages voted unanimously," Garrick said.

"You should be ashamed of yourself, Garrick." Reynard pointed his finger at him. "You in particular should understand how that vote was made in the heat of battle. And after Sunathri …"

Garrick waited while Reynard collected himself.

Memories came to him. Sunathri's voice soft, yet firm, her eyes blazing with commitment, the touch of her hand as they joined in spell casting. Garrick, like all of the Freeborn, was here because of Sunathri's vision and the power of her beliefs. Yet her memory also made his hunger twist. It was a hunger he was learning to control, or at least to exist with, but it was still a blackness, dark and malignant, that still seeded his dreams with images of the two women he thought he had loved, both now dead because of him. And it was a hunger that was growing as restless as he was.

"Sunathri is dead," he said.

"And if she wasn't, then what Darien is doing to her order would surely accomplish the job."

"Do you think she would have wanted us to be bickering like this?"

"Sunathri would do what it took to drive her vision."

"No," Garrick's reply was, perhaps, too sharp. "Sunathri would do what it took to keep the Freeborn together. There is a difference."

"If we use Darien's plan, nothing will ever get developed."

"Darien's structure *is* a tightly reined approach," Garrick admitted.

It was, in fact, a bureaucratic nightmare that he and Darien had argued over in private for each of the past three nights—an argument that contributed to his headache this morning and hence his jaunt to the practice range. The fact that Garrick had healed Darien's father—to the extent possible, anyway—had not given Darien any mind to bend from his position. He believed the people of Dorfort needed to see the order as being constrained or they would never accept the Freeborn as a full partner in their midst.

Reynard spoke in a firm voice.

"The orders aren't dead, Garrick. You've said so yourself. We have to be strong enough to defend ourselves when they decide to finish the job they started. This approach of development by committee that Darien wants to create will kill our progress."

Garrick sighed.

Reynard wasn't much older than Garrick was. But where Garrick just wanted to find his own way in his new world, Reynard was full of vision, ready to tackle the entire plane. He pushed ideas before him as if they were cut diamonds, fully expecting Garrick and Darien to be dazzled by their brilliance.

That was the problem with the entirety of the Torean House today. They were comprised of mages who were, by nature, independent and opinionated. They did not follow rules and they were used to doing as they pleased. That was no surprise, of course. If Toreans dealt well with organization they would likely already have been in an order to begin with. But unions required rules and restrictions, and when it came to defining these rules, members of the Torean House were like a gang of roosters in a hen house.

"What do you really want?" Garrick finally said.

"I want you to lead the Freeborn."

"And if I were ever to agree to that, and then *I* did not do as you think necessary, would you not just attempt to dispose of me like you're trying to dispose of Darien?"

"It's not like that."

"Isn't it?"

"I only want what's good for the mages."

"The mages asked Darien to lead them."

"You should get out among them more often, Garrick."

"What's that supposed to mean?"

Reynard paused, then thought better. "I'm sorry," he said. "That was too firm. But Darien has squandered his goodwill. The mages are bickering. They think electing Darien was a mistake."

Garrick grimaced. "Go away, Reynard," he said.

"We need to resolve this."

"There's nothing to resolve. If you want what's best for the mages, you'll stop throwing oil on this fire—and when they grumble, you'll tell them Darien is a good man who means nothing but the best."

Garrick hefted the bow and reached for another practice bolt. He nocked the arrow against the bow's taut gut and faced the target, feeling Reynard's gaze. Sweat rolled into one eye. He blinked it away, but still his vision swam. Swordplay rang out from across the field. A breeze blew a single strand of Garrick's hair over his cheek. The target stood across the field. The bolt was long, the weapon's pull strong. He concentrated on the black mark at the target's center and let fly.

The bolt swept wide.

"As I said," Reynard muttered. "Your apprentice is a better shot than you'll ever be."

He turned then and walked across the field.

Garrick was still steaming as he stepped into his chamber —a large suite with a view that overlooked Blue Lake.

Will whirled as Garrick entered. The boy had been facing away from him and bent inquisitively over a table in the middle of the room. He held one hand behind his back.

"Garrick, sir?" Will said with guilt crawling over his expression. The boy was dressed in a baggy linen overshirt and breeches that had been dirtied at the knees.

"What are you up to now?" Garrick said, slamming the door with more force than necessary.

"Uh ..."

Will's gaze fell to the floor. His hand came forward, holding a small lab book. The words *Mice and Other Small Rodents* were penned on the cover in dark ink.

Alistair, Garrick's previous superior, had kept this journal, and many just like it, for years. They were filled with jotted notes and pages of experimental spellwork. Darien had retrieved them from the ruins of Alistair's manor and presented them to Garrick as a gift after the events at God's Tower.

"How many times do I have to tell you I'll begin your training after things settle?"

"I'm sorry," Will said.

Garrick held his hand out. "Give me the book."

Will handed it to him.

He ran his fingertips over the worn leather binding. The edges were rough, ragged, and torn with use. Thin cracks crept over the cover like a spider web spun by time. He riffled through the pages, noting diagrams and sketches. Was it only last spring that Garrick had been a simple apprentice?

He looked at Will.

"Are the horses exercised?"

"Yes, sir."

"Groomed and fed?"

Will nodded, his dark eyes widened in a "you can believe me" gaze.

"How about lunch?"

"You didn't say anything about lunch."

Garrick laughed. "Your stomach alone should be enough to tell you when to get lunch around."

"I'm sorry, sir."

"Not to worry. I expect Daventry will still have something in the kitchen. Turkey, probably. Get some for both of us—with bread."

"Yes, sir."

Will slipped past him, and the door shut gently.

A quiet settled around him.

Outside his window, tall ships lay in Dorfort's port and men unloaded crates of goods from distant places like Whitestone and Farvane. He put the book back on the table and cast his glance around the chamber. It was larger than any dwelling he had ever occupied before. A padded velour couch ran along the far wall. A desk filled one corner. A connecting room held the library of Alistair's journals. His bed chamber connected from the other side, linens freshly made and scented with spices from lands to the east.

Such luxury made him uncomfortable.

A knock came to his door.

It would be Will, of course, coming back to double-check his order. The boy could never keep anything right. "Turkey!" he yelled as he whirled. "With bread."

The door swung inward.

Darien stuck his head through the opening.

"I've been called worse, I suppose," he said with a grin. "But I tend to think of myself as grain-fed steak from Horval."

Garrick chuckled despite himself.

"I thought you were someone else."

"I saw the boy slinking out of here. Looked like a whipped pup."

Garrick sat on a chair and twisted his lips into a smirk. "I snapped at him."

Darien shut the door and took a seat at the edge of the couch. He wore a cape lined with gold thread, a freshly cleaned tunic, and a wide belt polished to a black shine. His boots were spotless. His dark beard had come in fully throughout the months of summer. "He's a lot like you were, isn't he?" he said.

"Yes," Garrick replied. "He is." He leaned against the windowsill. "How is your father doing?"

"No change. Your cure has kept him alive, but he is still weak."

"He's a strong man, Darien. But my healing can only go so far. I don't think I can make anyone immortal."

"I know," Darien said, though his eyes displayed a combination of hurt and confusion that let Garrick know Darien could not possibly understand. "We will see what happens."

"I'm sorry to have left him that way," Garrick said. "It was all I know to do."

"He was happy to see you, you know?"

Garrick didn't completely agree on that point, but he nodded rather than argue. "To what do I owe this visit?" he said.

Darien paused.

"I'm sorry about last night," he said. "Calling you scatter-brained was out of line."

"So, you've reconsidered your position on experimentation, and are now all for it?"

"No. But I apologize for losing my temper. I was tired, and it was late."

"You need to trust me on this one Darien."

"I do. I trust you."

"No, you don't. You're not listening. I came here at your request. I gave your father his cure—"

"Just because you saved my father's life does not mean I will cave to your wishes when it comes to the people of Dorfort."

Garrick's face flared with heat, and his head throbbed. "Don't twist my words, Darien. We've been together too long for that. I didn't cure your father as a bargaining chip."

Darien nodded. "I'm sorry for my insinuation."

The two sat in silence for a moment.

"The mages need to test their work, Darien."

"And they can."

"But they won't do it under your plan. You can't expect to approve every step they take."

"That is nonsensical."

Garrick felt discomfort rise within him. "Nonsensical" had become Darien's favorite word, and he said it with that lilt to his voice, that tiny edge that said it wasn't really the idea that was nonsensical, but the person instead.

"The city is on edge, Garrick. Surely you see that? Despite all of your efforts to save lives, it is a fact that we lost good people at God's Tower. And our citizens want to see something come of it. They were sympathetic to the Torean cause because the Freeborn were the downtrodden, and because the Lectodinians and Koradictines were clearly a threat. But everything is different now."

"Not everything," Garrick said. "We both know the orders are still dangerous. The citizens of this city may have taken a dislike to the Freeborn, and they may be leery of my rumored powers—" he held up a hand to cut off Darien's arguments "—I hear them, Darien. Don't pretend you don't. I know what people think of me. Children shrink away as I walk down the streets, and I hear stories of how I tore souls straight from living bodies—all of them true, I might add. I hear them question if I am a mage or a demon, and to be truthful I can't blame them because I ask myself the same questions when I gaze into the mirror."

He paused.

"None of this, however, matters to the Koradictines or the Lectodinians, who *will* return, and none of it matters to the Torean mage who wants to experiment."

"If the Torean House doesn't put controls in place, the people will see to it that it does matter."

Garrick groaned as his hunger pressed against its bounds again. "I'm sure you didn't come up here to cover the same arguments over again," he said. "What do you want?"

"I need the council to be able to approve all experimental practices, Garrick. Without this, the people of Dorfort will not accept the Freeborn. And if the people of Dorfort don't accept them, then no one else will, either."

"You don't understand mages, Darien. They don't care if people accept them or not."

"Then maybe it's a good thing I don't understand mages, because it's obvious that mages don't understand the average citizen of Dorfort."

Garrick turned to gaze idly out the window. His hunger was still rising, his head swirling, and his vision blurring. He stood and planted his hands on the sill, staring over the city. His fingers gripped the wood of the sill. Its coarse grain had been sanded and oiled over to protect it from rain and sun. The stone below it was hard and cold, but the wood was different, pliable in ways the stone wasn't. His fingers seemed to sink into the wood, his flesh molding to become one with it.

Blackness rose inside him.

Words echoed in his hearing—Braxidane's voice, twisted and distorted by distance.

The wood had been alive once. It had grown on a hillside with thousands of other trees, elm and oak, white birch that rose like living spikes into the sky.

"Are you all right?" Darien's voice broke in.

The image shattered.

Garrick pulled his hands from the sill. Yes. They were still his hands. The sill was still the sill. A shudder crossed his back.

"I said, are you all right?"

Darien was standing beside him with concern on his face.

"Yes," Garrick said, embarrassment coming over him. "I'm fine. I just need to rest."

"How long has it been?"

"I only slept a few hours last night."

"No. I meant how long have you been keeping yourself bottled? How long since you last fed?"

Garrick glanced warily at Darien, knowing exactly what his friend was asking.

"Are you worried I'll release wrath on the people?"

Darien's crestfallen face told him how wrong he had been.

"Don't pretend with me, either, Garrick. I know your powers as well as any man alive, and I think your inner essence clouds our entire discussion. You think a mage can't be expected to control his need to experiment because you can't control yourself. You're like a wolf. You pace and pace to walk off energy. You stay up at night, maybe howling at the moon for all I know. As a result, you think all of the other mages will balk at the controls I propose. But they're different, Garrick. I hold them to a different standard because they can decide what to work on and when to work on it.

Garrick leaned back against the wall and felt the brick hard against his spine. He rolled his head around his neck, trying to release tension.

"Darien, you are my friend, but your understanding of how Torean mages think is atrocious. Any Freeborn who was inclined to accept what you're proposing would already be a Lectodinian or Koradictine."

"You are a Torean, yet you accepted Alistair's direction."

"For the last time, Darien. There is an ocean of difference between a mentor and a legislator."

"Well," Darien said. "Either way, I think your magic is tearing you up right now."

"I can live with it," he said.

"I've seen what happens when it's been too long, Garrick. You can't just not deal with it."

A tiny knock came from the door.

"Come."

Will stepped through, carrying a tray of food covered with red linen. Silence hung awkwardly as the boy put the tray on the table.

"I'll leave you to your meal," Darien said, standing. "The next council meeting is tomorrow. I'm counting on you."

The rest of Darien's sentence was left unspoken, but Garrick understood clearly what Darien was saying—*without your support, the Freeborn will not accept the bylaws.*

Darien left.

The smell of food wafted from the tray.

"I'm sorry about Alistair's journal, sir," Will said, his face a clouded mix of contrition and desire. "I just wanted to learn something."

"It's all right, Will," Garrick said with a wave of his hand. "I'll begin teaching you sometime soon."

Will smiled.

"But for now, let's eat."

CHAPTER
SEVEN

"The plan is perfect," Neuma said with a flourish.

The rest of the Koradictine council was silent, a fact that made her even more confident. It *was* perfect. Ettril would request an audience with Lord Ellesadil in Dorfort, where he would point to his shattered order and ask for a peaceful coexistence. Such a meeting would certainly draw Darien and Garrick, putting those two out of the scenario. Fil would slip into the manor and cast a spell over any guards outside the stable. At the same time, Hirlenat and Quin Sar would encapsulate the entire area in magic that would hide their casting from any Torean mages outside the manor area. The encapsulation was the most difficult part, but it didn't have to be perfect—she would need only a moment to swoop into the stable area and grab the boy.

The plan took advantage of the perception that the Koradictine order was decimated. It allowed Ettril to be seen publicly during the event, meaning he could deny involvement if necessary. As long as Fil was gentle on the guards, no one else would be hurt, reducing Dorfort's ability to rouse outside support.

Yes, the plan was perfect in every way.

But she was banking on her compatriots to be leery of her, too. She knew they wouldn't trust her to perform her role all by herself.

That was the key element in *the rest* of her plan.

"Why wouldn't I cast a blanket spell that would put them *all* to sleep?" Fil asked.

"You mean the stable hands as well as the guards?"

"Yes."

"That would work, but if you cast a blanket, we could have people falling in the middle of corrals where they would be easily seen. I felt it safest to merely work on the guard."

"What happens if you can't grab the boy?" Hirl-enat said. "Or what if he's guarded more closely?"

"That's a good point," Neuma replied. "I'll need to have a spell prepared in case the boy's covered. Perhaps you could suggest a few yourself. I've considered several, but would be grateful for any thoughts you might have."

"That still doesn't account for cases where you might struggle to handle the boy. Even a short scuffle could destroy the timing."

"Perhaps Quin Sar could join Neuma after he finishes helping Hirl-enat with the encapsulation," said Ettril.

"I considered that, Superior," Neuma answered. "But I was concerned that putting too much strain on Hirl-enat's magic may cause problems. Holding encapsulation for that long will be difficult."

"I can do it," Hirl-enat snapped back.

Ettril nodded.

Quin Sar's glance bounced from the superior to Neuma to Hirl-enat. His distrust of Neuma was obvious and, of course, not without merit. "The timing would be very tricky."

"If I rest adequately beforehand, I can do the entire encapsulation," Hirl-enat offered.

Ettril gave him a disbelieving glance.

"I've cast more difficult spell work before," Hirl-enat said, drawing himself up in his chair.

Fil scratched his cheek. "If Hirl-enat can manage the encapsulation by himself, that *would* make snatching the boy considerably more certain."

"And, admittedly," Neuma added with reluctance she hoped seemed sincere, "the encapsulation shouldn't need to be held that long."

The superior cast a questioning glance at Quin Sar and received a thin-lipped nod in return.

"It's decided, then," Ettril said. "Quin Sar will accompany Neuma."

"Where will you take the boy?" Fil asked.

"Neuma and Quin Sar will bring him back here," Ettril responded before anyone else could. "I will handle it from that point."

Neuma grinned. "Whatever you decide at that point, superior, be prepared to do it immediately. Unless I miss my mark, Garrick will not be far behind."

"You'd best not miss your mark by far on that point, Neuma," Ettril replied. "Our entire plan is based on it.

"I have no fear, Lord Superior. Garrick will follow."

EIGHT

Braxidane cut a swath through Existence, brushing tendrils against gates, touching entire lands of people and moving energy into and out of those lands. He was careful, always careful. It would be unseemly to be caught violating an agreement he had brokered himself. But sometimes, if everything was right and none of the others were watching, he would extract just a tad more than he gave. He had a secret reservoir where he stored these extra gleanings, protected away, hidden from prying senses.

This time, however, he wasn't interested in extending his cache. This time he spread his filaments through Existence, enjoying its friction for the mere pleasure of the act. Yal, a plane of little magic, was perpetually balanced. Costaralan was still growing. Ragant had slipped toward chaos, and smelled vaguely of brother Pullini's influence.

A dark green shiver ran through him.

Pullini seemed to think the planes were there for his own entertainment. He constantly stretched the rules, pushing residents as far as the guidelines would allow and then sometimes further. Braxidane wouldn't mind it so much, but Pullini did nothing of any value with the extras he gleaned. Instead, he consumed and consumed, and when he went too far and got himself dragged before Joint Authority he always complained he was being persecuted.

Pullini was a coward.

Braxidane slipped through connective tissues between the planes, enjoying the process of travel despite the pall that brother Pullini put over him.

Rastella lie ahead, a world that he owned, and that—due to its direct link to Talin—was rich with highly evolved and elegantly crafted magic. He was interested in a mage there, a child still, but one showing talents as natural as Garrick's had been.

Braxidane reached for the gate, hoping for a taste of its unique flavor, and maybe the briefest update on the child. But it scalded him at his touch, and when he pulled the tendril back he smelled the odor of smoke.

He drew on media to heal the wound. Once the pain subsided, he triaged the damage. He had lost a chunk of himself, easily resolved by dipping into his node and pulling from his worlds. But as he touched the wounds, a sensation of dread filled him.

Hezarin.

Her flavoring was clear and unmistakable.

His sister had been busy.

She had taken over Rastella, and had warded it with powerful controls.

He hesitated, not wanting to confront her while he was still in pain. But this had to be done, and it was best to get it over with now. So Braxidane flowed until he drew close enough to spread himself around Hezarin's node. She was alone, relaxing languidly and soaking energy from the flow around her. Nervous tension built as he stepped through the membrane of her cell.

"I was wondering when you would come," Hezarin said.

"What are you doing?" Braxidane replied.

"What does it look like I'm doing, brother? I'm occupying my node and listening to the flow."

"You've taken Rastella."

"So?"

"I want it back."

She laughed. "Go away, Braxidane."

"Are you begging to be brought before Joint Authority?"

Hezarin's movement then was slow and graceful, like a sheet billowing in the spring breeze. She folded on herself, gathering from the outside until she stood with physical presence before him.

"I've committed no crime greater than you did when you entered Adruin to save your champion there."

He blanched.

"You didn't think I knew about that, did you?"

Braxidane was silent.

It was all some time ago. Garrick had been drowning, and if he had died Braxidane's efforts would have been for naught. Braxidane thought he had been subtle. He thought he had slipped into the plane without creating a ripple, and he thought his alteration was small enough to pass unnoticed—it was, after all, merely a single casting. He rationalized that saving Garrick then had not *directly* affected a battle, and therefore had not harmed the efforts of any other planewalker. But that argument would be unlikely to stand in Joint Authority any better than Hezarin's decision to take Rastella from him would.

"How did you find out?" he finally said.

Hezarin laughed again. "Put me up on Joint Authority if you wish, Braxidane. We'll share whatever punishments the collective decides to dole out."

"Be very careful playing this game, sister," Braxidane said. "There will be others who will notice, and many of them may be less ... motivated ... to give you leeway."

"Just the thought of you providing cautionary advice on how to make such arrangements makes me laugh."

"I'm serious."

Hezarin mocked him. "*I'm serious.*"

Ignoring her, Braxidane pressed on. "None of us in Existence are very good at following the agreement."

"Shocking, isn't it?"

"And there are a hundred such deals between us all—maybe a thousand."

"Are you done being boring, yet?"

"You don't see it, do you? All it takes is one agreement to break with enough vehemence, and a domino chain could cascade throughout All of Existence. One of us blows up and calls in an agreement on another, who, in turn, calls in their own chits. Let's not create another domino in the chain, sister. You've made your point. Now give me back Rastella."

"This is the best you can do, Braxidane? Seriously?"

"It should be enough."

"Go away," Hezarin said.

Braxidane waited for a moment, then, realizing it was a hopeless cause, he slipped out of Hezarin's node.

An unsettled taste flared within him. Hezarin wasn't going to back down, and if she controlled Rastella she was certain to discover his candidate. Braxidane returned to his node in a cloud of contemplation. He had to do something. This action from his sister could not be left to stand. He saw two options—let her have the plane and risk losing the mage, or take it back and risk what could turn out to be an ugly chain of events.

He spread out in his node, dipped his consciousness into the flow, and began to consider the possibilities.

Raucous voices echoed through Dorfort's royal ballroom—a cavernous grand hall that was often used for events of state, celebrations, and festivals. Garrick sat at the head of the table with Darien and Reynard. Mages filled the rest of the seats. Will and several apprentices cleared plates and filled mugs.

Arabel, a mage of some respect, spoke. "Even if we grant the council needs to oversee all research, how can we create proposals if we can't experiment to decide what's achievable?" He sat down in a huff, smoothing his robes and twisting his beard as the rest of the mages buzzed with agreement.

This wasn't going to be good, Garrick saw.

Darien dabbed at the corner of his mouth, then placed the cloth napkin beside a plate that held the remains of his roasted cormorant.

"I understand, Arabel. This oversight board *will* slow the development of magic. But *both* my advisors have told me progress can be attained in this fashion."

"That's horse dung," Elaina, a sorceress from the northeastern ranges, said. "Just because something is achievable, does not mean it is wise."

Mages grumbled their assent.

Darien replied. "I understand why you would say that, but this is important. The House of the Freeborn needs to be aligned to the city, and, despite that the people of Dorfort are among the most enlightened citizens on the plane, they still fear you. You have to face the fact that they tolerate the presence of this order today only because I have given them my assurances. This approach will change their perspective of the order."

"What we do will make their lives easier," Elaina replied. "If they can't see that, then they don't matter."

"That is the attitude that created the citizens' fear of the orders to begin with," Darien said. "I want our house to leverage the talents of all its members to help the common good. That was Sunathri's vision, after all. We all want that. If a mage finds a spell that protects against disease and aging, it is of no use unless people are willing to endure it."

Darien paused to let the audience consider his point.

"What we're arguing about is really just a matter of time," he finally said.

"Time?"

"Yes. Trivial, really. If we constrain ourselves today, the population will accept us. As that occurs I foresee a time when we can release these self-imposed constraints. Can you all see that vision? Can we agree that this is the true situation?"

Two mages toward the back of the room stood, scowls pasted on their faces. Boots from the mages scraped discordantly against the polished floor, and the ceramic clatter of plates being pushed along bare tabletops created a collage of sound that said the Freeborn most definitely did not see anything at all like Darien suggested they should.

Elaina wrapped her walking shawl over her shoulders.

Voices rose.

The order was disbanding before Garrick's very eyes.

He stood without thinking, and the mages turned, quieting

almost as one. The pressure of their gazes was red heat against his hunger. Something stirred inside him, a fragrance—so brief, so brief—but it was her, wasn't it?

Sunathri.

It felt like it. Was it Sunathri's life force, turning inside him?

He didn't know.

"Which is better?" he said as he collected himself.

Expressions across the room grew quizzical, and motion came to a halt.

"To live in an order that advocates the careful application of magic, or to go it alone?" Garrick turned his hand out in supplication. He spoke almost without thinking, feeling oddly calm, sensing himself in the same role he had often watched Alistair provide as his superior had counseled other mages. "I don't know," he answered himself. "But that *is* the question on the table today. You see that, don't you? This is a question of whether we have an order or not.

"There will always be Torean wizardry. It was here before Sunathri came and bound you up together. It will be here long after we are all dead and gone. Her idea, though, was that a group of independent wizards could do such good work that, when they combined, people would love them. And she thought this connection between mage and citizen would change the world. Darien's proposal makes that connection paramount, it says the Freeborn will be part of the world no matter what. The counter position accentuates the portion of Sunathri's vision that is lodged in personal freedom, that a mage can make his or her own choice at all times, just as I did on the battlefields surrounding God's Tower, and just as I do today. I want you to see that. I want you to see that Darien holds no personal bias against magic. He wants it to flourish."

The mages grumbled, and Darien nodded.

"But I want Darien to see that a mage must be free to make their way. This is the message that must be sent to the public of Dorfort."

"Hear, hear," a mage said.

Garrick fought a surge from his hunger as he waited for the hall to quiet. His vision wavered, and he had to catch his breath. It was growing, that hunger. He had only a little time.

"So that question: how will the Torean House be built? How will it exist? Is a question you each have to ask yourself. And those answers feel to me like they could decide much in the course of history. I've been in the field recently. I know a little of what I speak. The Koradictines and Lectodinians are lying fallow, licking their wounds, but I can say for certain that they are not gone. The Lectodinians are still particularly strong. And if I make my mark, there will be more pain from these orders, and that pain will come sooner rather than later. Darien asked if you saw his version of the future as ringing true. I ask if you feel my version, also. I ask if you can see a future wherein it is deadly to be so independent that we are each alone."

Heads nodded.

Garrick opened his mouth to speak further.

He felt suddenly disoriented, and he clutched the table to avoid falling.

"I ..."

His vision blurred again, and pressure pounded against his forehead—he felt a wind, a lightness under his feet, a swirling in the hunger within him. Then he smelled the telltale scent of Braxidane's magic, heavy with the sickly sweet taste of sugar burnt on a griddle. He saw a tunnel billowing toward him, dark blue clouds turning like a cyclone.

"*Garrick?*"

It was Darien. His voice echoed from somewhere distant.

"Are you well, Lord Garrick?" Reynard said.

He felt Will coming toward him.

But mostly he felt Braxidane's pull, and as blackness crackled over his body and his hunger folded in on itself, the skin around his eyes grew tight with a gale of wind that grew to a banshee's howl.

"Stop!" he screamed, but knew the word was not audible.

Suddenly he was flying through air that was gray and silver.

TEN

Darien gasped.

In that moment, with all eyes upon him, Garrick disappeared.

Gone.

One moment he was there, standing before the house of the Torean Freeborn and laying the framework of a plan, then he was gone, blinked out of existence leaving nothing but his half-eaten lunch to show he had ever existed.

The mages became deathly silent. Then Elaina cleared her throat and bedlam ensued. Mages cried out, speaking to each other in rapid-fire bursts. Tables and chairs groaned. Ceramic plates clattered.

"The orders have taken him!" a voice yelled.

Reynard cast a quick spell to scry for danger but found apparently nothing. Another mage cast a shield over himself and a few others within his reach.

Darien stood, calling for calm that didn't come.

Finally, Reynard leapt to the table and cast a strobe of light. "Enough!"

The mages came to an abrupt quiet.

"What's happened?" Elaina asked.

"I don't know," Reynard responded. "But I motion we bring this discussion to a halt and break into groups to investigate."

"I agree," Darien said. "We need to find the truth."

The gathering seemed to accept this.

Reynard selected Elaina and three other mages.

"You'll help Darien and I work on a plan. The rest of you are excused for now. I want you all available at a moment's notice, though. We'll call our next session soon."

Arabel spoke.

"What if this is an attack? The orders could be at the city gates as we speak."

"If this were a full-out attack we would be hearing the horns blaring by now," Darien said. "But it could be a foreshadowing. So, I suggest Reynard lead our magical response while I go brief Lord Elle-sadil so he can prepare for defense."

Reynard nodded. "That seems wise."

Elaina sat down.

"All right, then," Darien said, pushing the sleeves of his tunic up to his elbows. "Let's get to it."

ELEVEN

"With all due respect, Lord Ellesadil," Darien said. "Garrick has gone missing and you're seriously considering the idea of granting a conference to the High Superior of the Koradictine order?"

Ellesadil, Lord of Dorfort, looked up from his desk with his quill in mid-air. The letter he had been composing—a response to the Koradictine proposal received earlier that morning—was unfinished on the desktop. A large opal gleamed from one finger, and a gold ring with the seal of the city embossed upon it glittered from another. Ellesadil was just past the midpoint of his life, yet his body was still trim, his hair just now streaking gray, and his eyes still full of youthful energy. He wore a white silk shirt from the southern marshlands that made his skin appear even more hale.

"How is your father, Darien?"

"Sir?"

Ellesadil put the quill down.

"Your father. I asked how he's doing."

Darien paused. "He won't eat, Lord. I fear we're seeing his last. The physician is with him daily, though."

"I'll stop by to see him."

"I'm sure he would honored, sir."

Ellesadil nodded.

"Again, though, Lord Ellesadil. You can't think that the appearance of the Koradictine request coming at this most inopportune of moments is pure coincidence."

"You suspect they are linked?"

Darien knit his brow and leaned forward, both palms on Ellesadil's desk. "Ettril Dor-Entfar is our enemy. Certainly the timing of this smells of deceit. I can't believe the two are mere coincidence."

"And, yet, I see no reason to believe they are linked. Garrick is not known for his stability, after all," Ellesadil said in an even voice. "I have every reason to believe he left of his own accord. And, let's be clear on one more thing, too. The Koradictine order is an enemy of the Torean Freeborn, not the people of Dorfort. We fought alongside you because it was the right thing to do, but now that your skirmish has been settled, I have no specific qualm with Ettril, nor do I consider what's left of the Koradictine order to be a threat."

"I understand your position, Lord," Darien said. "But I think you're being too simplistic. Many of our families lost members during the mage war. Meeting with Ettril will provide them with the wrong message."

"That depends on what is said."

Darien straightened with a bit too much flash. Papers flew from the desk in his wake as he turned toward the window.

"What are you trying to accomplish?" he said.

"Before I answer that, Darien, I suggest you take a moment to calm yourself."

Darien flushed, glancing out the window and down to the city. He remembered when the manor was built—a time when he was just a boy. Ellesadil had ordered the designers to change the direction of the window away from a view of the bay, as they had originally designed, and into a view of the city. "*Better to understand the people than the lake,*" the lord had said at the time.

Darien had admired that about Ellesadil.

Even Ellesadil's simplistic naming of his manor as the governing center spoke of his role as a manager rather than a king or other such maker of absolute law. Ellesadil's rule had always been one of even-handedness.

Darien took one of the padded seats beside the desk.

"I apologize for my rashness, sir."

"It is all right. Good men are often overzealous at times. I've had several such conversations with your father over the years."

"Thank you. It's just … I'm worried about this."

"How so?"

"Garrick's been gone for more than a week, sir."

"Yes," Ellesadil said. "I know that. And I also know the Freeborn are finding it difficult to come to agreements. Now, Ettril shows up at our doorstep, wanting to beg forgiveness. I can see why everyone involved with the Torean House would be anxious."

Darien sighed.

"I'm glad you understand," he said. "I just can't bring myself to trust the Koradictines. The whole thing smells strange, doesn't it?"

"Times today are always strange."

"May I ask what you're trying to accomplish by agreeing to this meeting?"

"That would be a natural question for the leader of the Freeborn to ask," Ellesadil said.

"And your answer?"

"I want to understand what Ettril is thinking. I want to know what his goals are."

"As well as to assess whether this man is trustworthy, I hope?"

"Of course."

"And what will such action say to the people of this land?"

"It will say we're willing to move forward," Ellesadil replied. "If the conversation goes well, it will say forgiveness is possible, and if it does not, it will say that their leadership was open to peaceful coex-istence."

Darien chewed his lip. "I understand."

"That's good." Ellesadil intertwined his fingers and put them together before him. "Now, maybe you can tell me more about Garrick."

"I don't know anything new. He disappeared before our eyes with no sign of a scuffle. Didn't take anything with him. Didn't leave a warning or a message. Our mages have searched and scried. We've scoured his room. Nothing. No remnants of magic beyond that in the hall itself."

Ellesadil sighed. "I have to admit that Garrick scares me in ways I can't begin to explain."

"I can't say I understand him that well, myself, Lord" Darien replied. "But I know he's a good man."

"You miss him."

Darien nodded. "It's especially hard with the boy."

"They are close, aren't they?"

"They are quite similar—so quiet. Will thinks Garrick left him, and that hurts him to his core."

"Do your best, Darien. It will work out. Your father raised you well."

"Thank you, Lord."

"Now, if you would, I have things to attend to before the day is out. If I'm forced to stay here too late, I'll miss the lady of state's dinner table."

Darien grinned. "Never a wise mistake to make."

"But one I fear has become too much of a habit."

Darien went to the door.

"Darien?" Ellesadil said before Darien could leave.

"Yes."

"I will want you to attend my discussion with the Koradictine leadership if you would."

Darien nodded. "Reynard should be there, also."

"Yes," Ellesadil said. "Well played."

"And Garrick. If he returns in time."

"Of course. If he returns in time."

TWELVE

Neuma flicked a bit of dead leaf from her sleeve as she prepared for their ride into Dorfort. Deciding to remain as nondescript as possible, she chose no jewelry and wore the brown tunic and heavy shirt of thick weave that Kathery had given her before the mage war. Her pants were black wool. It was nearing winter, and already the heavy smell of thick undergrowth had left the forest. She cut the chill further by slipping a riding cloak over her shoulders.

Outside her tent came the sounds of gathering. Horses nickered and their hooves clopped randomly as the boys made them ready.

The trip from de'Mayer island had been difficult. The weather crossing the ocean had been bad to start with and hadn't gotten any better until they managed the entirety of Badwall Pass, the long road that was the surest way of traversing the northwestern portion of the plane. Ettril had chosen to travel south from there, closer to the Wizardpeak ranges, rather than taking the eastern route along the Vapor Peaks. The Superior said he liked the southern pass due to its more plentiful game and the ease of its passage. But it was the longer way, and it required crossing a large river, so Neuma knew the choice had as much to do with the fact that the Lectodinian stronghold was somewhere in the Vapor Peaks as for any other reason.

It was, likely, a wise choice, though. The Koradictine order could probably not survive a conflict with the Lectodinians now.

To add to the hardship, Ettril was no longer a young man. The superior did not travel well. He was cranky and short-tempered on the best of days, downright spiteful the rest.

Hirl-enat was not much better.

A boy's voice came through the tent.

"Commanderess Neuma?"

"Yes," she replied, feeling a smirk cross her lips.

Hirl-enat had demanded titles for their trip, so Ettril had given them all the rank of commander. That, she thought, would be the first thing to go.

"Lord Superior Ettril would like a word."

"On my way," she said.

She slipped a stiletto into a sheath at her wrist, then rolled the sleeve of her shirt over it. Pulling her cloak tighter around her, Neuma stepped out of the tent.

Quin Sar was just emerging from his shelter.

Hirl-enat had left camp yesterday to prepare for his role.

Fil joined them, running his hands over his finest robes as they waited by the covered shelter Ettril demanded for himself.

Neuma smiled at them.

Her plan was coming to fruition.

THIRTEEN

Ettril Dor-Entfar, High Superior of the Koradictine order, entered Dorfort via the central road, riding in a carriage Lord Ellesadil had sent. He peered through its shuttered windows to find the street lined with on-lookers eager to get a glimpse of him. The ride came to a halt outside the government center. The press of people fell away under the Dorfort guard, then the carriage door swung open.

He motioned to Fil, and the younger mage made his exit first.

Then Ettril emerged from the carriage, resplendent in a bright robe of crimson, and carrying a staff made from a crooked span of gnarled driftwood from the ocean that surrounded de'Mayer island. He wore enough jewelry to dazzle the most active socialite, and he had combed his bushy beard so that it flared with silver fire in the afternoon sun.

With Fil escorting him, the Koradictine lord climbed the stairs to Dorfort's Governing Center.

Darien and Reynard, two of the three leaders of the Freeborn Torean House, waited for him to reach the top, then made formal introductions.

"Can we get you anything, High Superior?" said a member of the wait staff.

"Nothing for me, please. But my aide might be interested in a tour, or maybe even lunch."

"Lunch, sir?" the man asked Fil.

Fil gave a warm grin. "That would be nice. It was a very early breakfast."

"I imagine it was."

Darien stepped in. "Please do have Daventry arrange something. I'll ask Harol to meet him at the kitchen to escort Fil through the grounds after he's eaten."

"Thank you, Commander J'ravi," Ettril said.

With that, Fil was taken by the elbow and led away, and Darien and Reynard escorted Ettril to the central hall. Darien purposefully slowed his gait to match the Koradictine's. The walk was cool and awkward. "I hope your carriage was satisfactory, High Superior," Darien said.

"It was marvelous."

Reynard remained silent as their footsteps echoed down the hall-way. Eventually, they came to the meeting chamber where Ellesadil sat waiting.

"Lord Ellesadil," Darien said, "please meet Ettril Dor-Entfar, High Superior of the Koradictine Order of mages. High Superior, please meet Kandor Ellesadil, Lord Governor of Dorfort."

The two clasped hands.

Ellesadil was dressed in green and blue, wearing a thin shirt of polished chain mail under an overcoat marked with the insignia of the Dorfort guard. He greeted the High Superior with a cordial calm.

"So," Ellesadil said once each member of the party had been seated. "To what do we owe this pleasure?"

Now, all eyes were on Ettril.

"I expected the Torean god-touched mage would participate in our discussion," the Koradictine said.

"Garrick is unable to join us," Darien replied. "But I've asked

Reynard of the Freeborn to sit with us so he is conversant with what-ever issues we discuss."

Ettril nodded. This was interesting. The Torean god-touched mage was unavailable. Ettril wasn't sure what to make of it, but one thing was certain—something was amiss with the them. Garrick would not miss this if he could have attended. This could bode well.

Ettril began.

"I've come," he said. "To see what can be done about mending the damage my order has done throughout this plane."

Hirl-enat watched the parade while standing in the dining area of the inn across from Ellesadil's manor. When Ettril left the carriage, he stepped with unhurried gait back to the room he had taken the day before—a small compartment on the inn's second floor.

He shut the door behind him and closed the latch, then went to the window and pulled a pair of frayed curtains more fully shut. Thin light penetrated their linen sheen, but nothing else.

Hirl-enat, alone now, was ready to cast his spell.

He lit a candle and put it on a ceramic plate that sat on the floor at the center of the room, then he pushed the bed and a nondescript secretary to one corner. From the secretary, he removed two containers of paint he had prepared the night before. In short order, the floor was covered with runes.

He left the jars by the water pot.

The chambermaid would be upset when she came tomorrow, but by then it would be too late.

Hirl-enat placed smaller candles at key points of his pattern, then used the central candle to light them. He stepped carefully to avoid smudging his work. It would be disaster to rub out a rune with a poorly placed foot. The diagram was a half circle that filled most of the floor, open toward the manor. Looping sigils twined along the outer edge, representing the chaos that would exist outside the shell. Straight lines radiated from the focus of the half circle to denote stability within.

If he cast this spell correctly, it would hide all sorcery made within his range. And the range he had set out last night would cover Dorfort's government center, enough of it, anyway, that Fil's casting could be made unobserved by those outside the area, giving them all time to extract themselves if the plan worked.

And Hirl-enat saw no reason it shouldn't work.

His casting was old magic, filled with structure and componentry, and an elegance that made his mind settle. It was magic taught to him by his superior back in his days of youth, a crotchety old man named Kass with a similar passion for structure and a love of tradition. Hirl-enat was Kass's last apprentice, and the old mage had demanded nothing but the best of him.

He laid the spell out in methodical perfection.

Today's magic relied more often than not on short bursts of power rather than controlled processes. It was a change that scared him. Of course, he had—throughout his life—found that some in his order considered his thoughts regarding the value of structure in his casting to be Lectodinian in nature. When he was younger such accusations caused him to blanch, and he would sometimes prepare intricate revenge against those who made the claims. But he was older now. He understood certain truths he hadn't understood then. Nothing about Lectodinian politics made any sense, but that didn't preclude them from being right in one fashion. Sorcery should be an art rather than a convenience. Or, if not an art, a science, at least.

He licked his lips then. They were dry and chapped, an old man's lips, he thought. When did he come to have an old man's lips?

Hirl-enat shook his mind of these ruminations and began instead to prepare himself.

Not everyone could hold the encapsulation for long enough to complete the kidnapping. Ettril would understand this fact. If the exercise succeeded he would be in the High Superior's favor for a very long time.

He took his place in the diagram and spoke his words of old magic, stepping across the floor in a dance-like pattern. The room filled with the gloriously bloody smell of Koradictine magic. And Hirl-enat threw his head back to enjoy the rapture of magestuff as it burned through his body.

Across the manor yard, an invisible shell formed over Dorfort's government center.

FOURTEEN

The guard leading Fil to the kitchen was young and trying perhaps too hard to impress him. He went out of his way to talk about each of the tapestries that hung on the walls, giving the full history of both the artist and the stories behind the artwork's origin. Fil thought them merely over-wrought.

A wave of heat that smelled of baking bread hit before they arrived at the kitchen. The smell of freshly diced celery and stewing onions came next, a combination that did tricks inside his stomach. For the briefest of moments, he forgot he was nervous.

"Good afternoon, Daventry," the guard said. "This is Fil, mage of the Koradictine order. He is in need of a quick lunch."

The cook stood over an open grill and wiped his hands on a clean rag. Three others chopped vegetables and cleaned cook pots. Lunch would be served in the royal hall and dinner would come soon enough, so this request was additional work in a room full of people who had plenty to do.

"It was a very early breakfast," Fil explained in hopes his apology came through.

"All right, then," Daventry said. "Let's see what we can rustle up."

He was a cheerful man with ruddy redness in his cheeks and a bare wisp of hair that was damp with sweat. His cheeks were made for a man bigger than himself. They spilled over his jawline like those of a bulldog, but a grin seemed to be perpetually pasted to his face.

The kitchen was laid out in the shape of a letter L.

The central nook consisted of a long grill and an open pit with a kettle and a roasting stand. A large hood opened to a chimney, its stone and mortared surface blackened by years of greasy smoke. A row of working ovens belched heat from the shortest wall. A longer counter was cluttered with rows of pots, pans, graters, and other utensils that looked like implements of torture.

Fil's eyes strayed to the bay windows that opened to view the manor.

"Those are Lord Ellesadil's stables," the guard explained.

"How many horses does he keep?" Fil asked. He wanted to keep the guard talking.

"It varies with the time of year. Ellesadil's policy is that any man who needs a horse can have one. But he must give his word for its return. So, early in the summer season, we're often left with a bare few. This time of year, though, the stables are nearly full."

The building across the manor was large. There were four others of similar size. Two guards per building. Ten people. Each would need to be unconscious for as much as half an hour.

"I had heard of your lord's generosity before," Fil said, "but was never sure if the stories were true or not."

"Oh, they're true, all right. I would follow Lord Ellesadil anywhere."

"That speaks volumes all to itself."

The guard smiled.

Fil lowered his voice. "Before your cook finishes gathering my meal, would you be able to show me to a privy?"

The guard's smile widened.

"This way," he said, leading him out the doorway and to a small room adjacent to the stables.

Hoping to avoid the guard's most intense scrutiny, Neuma and Quin Sar had entered the manor yard in the dark hours of early morning. They were simply dressed, giving the appearance of merely two citizens coming to the manor to barter with the blacksmiths, farmers, and tailors within.

Now they stood in a gathering bidding on pigs.

As hands raised and voices called prices, Neuma watched the guard lead Fil to the privy. With a sideways glance she saw Quin Sar's eyes glitter and watched a smirk cross his face. That smirk gave Neuma an understanding of something important. Quin Sar hadn't actually believed Fil would be able to get into position to cast his spell. He hadn't thought the plan would work.

Neuma's mind spun.

Quin Sar stood with a steely gaze. Only a few lines marked his cheeks and the corners of his eyes, and only a single brown age mark appeared on his jawline under his left ear, but he was older than his face let on. She had never considered Quin Sar's story much. He was a given, Ettril's second, his right hand—a man who had risen to his peak with careful application of loyalty. But this single expression brought her a new insight. If the superior's second had considered Neuma's plan a dog, why would he let it go forward without comment? Did Quin Sar have ambitions she hadn't taken into account?

Her veins ran cold. Maybe she should consider alternate plans, maybe send Quin Sar in alone? No. It was too late to swap horses now. Quin Sar may have plans of his own, but Neuma would press on and play whatever angle she was given when the time came.

This clarity calmed her nerves. She could handle anything as long as she was prepared.

Their line of sight gave Neuma a good view of the stables, good enough to see the boy, Will, anyway.

He was tall for his age, gangly. His body was mostly elbows and knees. He was assigned to the primary stable and had gone into and out of the hay room several times with pitchforks full of straw. The boy was concerned for something, though. Neuma could tell it by the way his round-eyed gaze kept returning every few minutes to a specific window high up on the manor.

Quin Sar noticed it, too.

Neuma wanted to know what was in that room, but she couldn't see into it well enough to get any ideas.

In the distance, Fil left the privy.

She looked immediately to the guards who had been seated just inside the stable. Both lay back, heads lolling against the wall in relaxed sleep.

"Come on," Neuma said, touching Quin Sar on the thigh, feeling the pressure of the wrist sheaths under the sleeves of her shirt as the two of them stepped away from the gathering, and went to the stable.

Now she was concerned only that Hirl-enat's part went well.

"THANK YOU," Fil said to his escort. "I feel much better."

The guard proffered a plate of tuna and cheese. "I understand completely. If you would like, you can eat as we walk."

"That would be excellent," Fil replied.

The truth was that Fil felt considerably more anxious now.

The spell was cast. Now the rest of his role consisted of waiting and hoping he didn't hear the excited exclamations that would mean the plan had failed, for if it failed, things would get difficult quickly.

Movement, he thought, would help calm the nerves.

Daventry hated the idea of giving any Koradictine mage access to the kitchen, better yet a plate of tuna. But Ellesadil had been clear that they were to treat these visitors well. He mopped his forehead with a towel, glancing at the doorway the mage and his escorts had just disappeared through. The door still swung on its hinges.

This mage was an odd one, as if any of them were not.

But this one seemed to be particularly on edge. Understandable, he supposed. Walking into an adversary's city had to be unnerving. But the mage's gaze had been like a water bug, never seeming to stay anywhere for long.

He shook his head. It was not his problem.

His problem had to do with these carrots that were laid out on the chopping table.

"Caro!" he called, snapping out of his cloud of thought and turning to a young woman who was hovering over an oven. "How many times do I have to tell you that I need the carrots sliced lengthwise today!"

She threw her hands in the air, but agreed to do them afresh. Daventry grumbled. Kitchen *workers* were easy to find. Kitchen *help*, on the other hand ...

He stepped outside and headed to the privy.

Neuma stepped casually past the unconscious guards, Quin Sar did the same at her side.

The stable was longer than it was wide, the entrance standing at the end of the longer dimension. The building inside was open and airy, though it still smelled of manure and hay. The stalls were made of wooden beams. Leather harnesses and rakes hung from stakes that had been pounded into the walls. Body heat from the horses made the place warmly pleasant after the chill of the open manor yard. The roof was open and buttressed by spans of rough-cut lumber that gave the place a simple, yet powerful feeling.

Two stable boys were attending a mare in the far portion of the stable. One boy was a young lad, maybe six or seven by Neuma's guess.

The other was Will.

Quin Sar raised a hand and twisted his ring finger into his palm. He whispered magic, and the two boys fell unconscious to the ground.

Neuma moved without thinking.

A flick of the wrist, and cold steel fell into her hand. The stiletto slid between Quin Sar's ribs, six inches of blade protruding into the mage's chest cavity.

Blood seeped.

Quin Sar's eyes widened, and he gave a pinched, choking sound as he struggled to get away. But Neuma drove him to the ground, silently stabbing again, and again.

When she was done, Quin Sar lay motionless on the ground, and she panted with her exertion.

"I'm sorry, old man. But you were in the way."

In more ways than one, Neuma thought. She could never truly run the order with Quin Sar alive.

She worked quickly from that point, dragging Quin Sar to where the boys lay, and leaving him beside the youngest. She pressed the stiletto into the boy's hand. Her wrist sheath needed to be wrapped twice around the boy's thin arm to get it to stay in place.

The sound of footsteps came from around a corner.

Calmly, she glanced at the area where she and Quin Sar had struggled. There were obvious signs of the skirmish, but she had no time to clean up that evidence.

She grabbed Will under the armpits and lifted him up.

Under the dead weight of sleep, the boy was heavy, but she could manage. She dragged him into a stall and hid behind a stack of bundled hay just as the footsteps rounded the corner. Neuma peered around the stack, set gates, and reached for her link to the plane of magic.

Two more hands entered the building—a young boy and a girl.

"What's that?" the girl said. She strode to where the boy and Quin Sar lay. "Dane?" she said.

The boy caught up to her.

"Dane!"

She reached down and touched the sleeping stable boy's temple, then yanked her hand back with a sick expression as she saw the bloodied blade and realized Quin Sar was dead. She stammered something Neuma couldn't hear and backed away with a face that grew more ashen every moment.

The boy looked around.

"Will?" he said. "Where's Will?"

The two looked at each other, eyes growing wider.

"Come on," the boy said as he grabbed the girl's wrist. "We've got to get help."

They ran out of the stable.

Knowing she had very little time, Neuma grabbed a rake from the wall and raced to remove the evidence of her struggle with Quin Sar. Four strokes removed the marks made by Quin Sar's heels as she had dragged him along. There was not much to be done for the thin splotches of blood that littered the area. With luck, they would appear to have been the result of random splatter rather than a dragging.

Having done the best she could, Neuma tossed the rake against the wall and ran back to Will. She hefted the sleeping boy over her shoulder and cast a quick illusion over herself. The image had flaws but should be good enough to keep the unprepared from seeing Will. Her vision tunneled, seeing only the door as she struggled toward it.

She shouldered the boy's weight again. Will's foot crashed against the doorway as she turned the corner a bit too quickly.

Their horses were in the alley across the street.

Neuma couldn't help holding her breath as she stepped carefully to the animals.

Her shoulder ached, and it was nearly impossible to get the boy slid up over her horse. But she managed. A moment later, she had mounted up and was leading her animal along a direct path out of the city, the boy still hidden in her illusion, and Quin Sar's horse following beside.

It was done, she thought. They had the boy.

Nothing else mattered.

Not really.

Ettril would succeed or fail.

Either way, she was ready.

And, either way, Garrick was sure to follow.

Coming back to the kitchen, Daventry scratched his head in wonder. The privy had smelled something awful, worse than the normal lavatory smell. It was like a meat locker, reeking powerfully of blood. He didn't know what to think of it.

Strange, but what could he say?

Who would care?

Stepping back into the heat of the kitchen, Daventry glanced at the young man who was cleaning the cookware.

"Clay," he yelled. "You don't clean wrought iron with water!"

Yes, kitchen workers were everywhere, but kitchen *help* ...

RASTELLA

FIFTEEN

Garrick pried open his eyes. He lay with his cheek pressed flat against hard stone. His body ached. His head throbbed. His mouth felt like it was filled with wool. He rolled to his side, then sat up and ran his hand through his hair. The wind here was cold and dry. Clouds of lavender and scarlet stretched across a panorama of rock that stretched as far as he could see. There was a faint scent about the place, the reek of wine left out overnight. In the distance, a thick band of brown smoke rose into the darkened sky.

A water skin and a rune-encrusted sword lay on the stone beside him.

Where was he?

What was Braxidane up to?

He stood up, swaying until he got his bearings.

He wore Torean black—a sleeveless tunic and breeches tucked into a pair of soft boots. He flexed his fingers, feeling the ache of muscle all the way up his arms. Oddly, his hunger was far away.

"What do you want?" Garrick called aloud, expecting Braxidane could hear him.

The wind carried his voice, but no one answered.

"Braxidane!"

Still nothing.

Garrick scowled. His skin prickled with the shrill wind. He had learned the hard way that his superior could be fickle, that Braxidane would pick and choose his own time and place for meetings. It made him angry.

He picked up the water skin and sniffed its contents.

The drink had a sugary aroma.

He sipped. It tasted good, so he drank.

The sword was the length of his forearm and had a curved blade that was etched with flowing rune work he could not read. He held it for a moment—feeling a power within that he could not define—then he placed it in a sheath he found a short distance away.

This he hitched to his belt.

Were the water and the blade gifts from Braxidane? He didn't know, nor at this time did he particularly care.

The column of smoke still marked the horizon.

Garrick didn't trust Braxidane, and he hated the idea of following the obvious. But his superior held all the cards in this game, and finding the source of the smoke seemed the best way to orient himself. Perhaps it was a city. So he took a final draught of the water, cursed Braxidane's meddling, and headed toward the column.

As he walked, a snarling growl came from over his shoulder.

He spun, but not in time to slip under the hurling white weight that struck him high on the shoulder. The beast was huge and cat-like, its teeth were gnarled fangs stained yellow and purple, and its claws extended like daggers.

Garrick rolled to the ground and reached for his link to the plane of magic, trying to set a gate. There was nothing there, though. No gate, no rushing current of Talin's magestuff. He felt nothing except the bitter wind and the burn of his hunger as it boiled beneath the surface of his mind.

The cat's fur stood on end as it hunched down, then leaped.

Garrick dodged, but the beast's claw ripped along his ribcage. The cat growled in triumph and turned, barring its purple teeth once again.

He reached for the sword and felt it pulse with the familiar tang of magestuff. It was a source, Garrick thought, a store of magical energy.

The cat struck again.

This time Garrick was quick enough to slice across its chest, bringing a vivid blue line of blood over its white fur. The cat's scream was as coarse as shattering rock. The smell of its blood pulled on Garrick's hunger.

He set a new gate, and this time magestuff flowed through the blade like a river.

The cat sniffed the wind, the folds above its nose gathering in fleshy mounds.

Garrick threw the sword with a simple, overhand motion, and the weapon flew gracefully, looping once before it buried itself deeply into the creature's chest.

It was dead before it hit the ground.

Garrick stood straight to catch his breath.

He glanced at the city ahead. He was close enough to see it was made of crystalline structures and awkward architectures that were like no city he had ever seen before. Then he looked at the corpse below, and finally at the garish purple and green sky above.

What was this place?

He withdrew the blade from the creature and felt the weapon sing. Power surged inside it. The blade twisted and twined as magic healed the wound at his side. He gritted his teeth until the pain faded, then he examined the sword. Though he still could not read them, the runes felt familiar.

It was Braxidane's blade. That much was certain. And it was somehow tied to the plane of magic.

He held the sword and set a gate that fell into place.

Yes.

He was right.

This plane was somehow blocked from Talin's flow, but the sword bypassed that and gave him a link. Garrick knew Braxidane better than to assume he would play fair and proper, though. The question now was to determine what game the planewalker was playing.

"What have you done, Braxidane?" he said to the wind. "Where have you taken me?"

The column of smoke still rose over the city.

A streak of lightning flashed from within, and a beacon of light encircled him with a mustard-yellow intensity. Ghostly shapes appeared on the surrounding rocks, solidifying into beings that looked like over-large men, each similarly dressed in cross-banded pants and billowing shirts of purple and brown. Noting the intensity of their gazes, Garrick's hunger rose, firm and strong, and he knew without counting that they numbered twenty.

"Who are you?" the man closest to Garrick said.

He was a giant figure, maybe half again taller than Garrick and seeming even taller still as he stood on a boulder that was already above Garrick's eye level. A ragged cape of animal hide draped over his shoulder and whumped like a sail in the breeze. He wore a helmet made of curved bone. But what struck Garrick most was that the man had three eyes set in a triangle on his forehead, the pupils glittering like amethyst.

"My name is Garrick."

"You're a wizard."

"What of it?"

The man waved a hand, and each of the twenty spoke magic.

Garrick pulled life force up in response.

Clouds of black and crimson closed in from above.

Garrick reached into his hunger and took a life.

The voices of the remaining mages combined, their magic stronger together than it had been apart. The air turned sour. He reached out to harvest more life force, grasping his sword and feeling the heat of runes flaring as he set gates and funneled bursts of magic into the fray.

Mages died.

Blackness swirled inside him. But it was not enough. His magic was slow here, and he couldn't stop the combined power of the three-eyed mages.

The air thickened with their presence, and Garrick fell to his knees under the onslaught, feeling the pressure of their sorcery with a weight like molten steel.

The last thing he remembered was the ground rushing at him.

CHAPTER

SIXTEEN

Chains bit into Garrick's wrists. His knees were pressed into the floor. Hard stone dug into the small of his back. His elbows were hyperextended and stiff from having hung unconscious for an excruciatingly long time. His head lolled forward, his shoulders twisted back. His feet were bare and numb, and his shirt had been removed, allowing the sweat to trickle down his back and chest in tingling rivulets of torture. His hair hung over his face like a veil, dirty and matted.

A trail of spittle dribbled from his slack jaw.

What was Braxidane doing?

Why was he meddling again?

As he came to his senses, Garrick tried to understand what was happening. He peered through blurred vision and dim lighting to see a hall that was vast and vaguely rectangular. People milled around him as if he was at a bazaar. The air was stifling with the heat of human bodies. He twisted in his shackles, and his hunger gave a sluggish churn, its movement labored like a fish swimming through stew.

He looked for his sword.

"T'aint here."

The huge, three-eyed man he had met in the field of boulders sat on a stool a distance away, a block of wood in one hand and a carving knife in the other.

"What's that?" Garrick said.

"Your weapon. T'aint here."

Garrick flexed his muscles, but chains still held his hands above his head. He could not bring his ankles together. He could stand, though. The chains clanked as he did so. The rush of blood made his feet feel like he was standing on briars.

"Where am I?" Garrick finally said.

The big man chuckled. The eye in the middle of his forehead glanced out over the crowd.

Garrick now recognized this massive hall of chaos for the marketplace it most certainly was.

Buyers milled about, examining men and women—prisoners chained to the wall or suspended from the ceiling in iron cages. Some of them slept. Others yelled, cursed, or groaned in various stages of lucidity. Their voices knit themselves into a steady blanket of noise that echoed across the expanse.

"This one is interesting," a female voice said, stopping before him.

She was smaller than the giant, and she had only two eyes, both of which were brown and both of which sized him up as if he were a cabbage.

"He's too small," said her partner, another woman, younger. "Won't last a cycle in the field."

The woman gave a snort and laid her hand on Garrick's wiry bicep. "I wasn't thinking about using him in the field."

"You're disgusting, Matla."

"He's not for sale, anyway," the three-eyed mage said. "I brought him here specifically for Lord Karasacti."

The woman frowned but moved on.

A new buzz came from the floor, and Garrick's hunger twisted like a netted shark. A curtain of people parted, leaving a clear view of a man in blue robes being escorted by two others—a man and a woman in robes of lighter blue. A metallic jangle accompanied their stride, growing sharper as they came nearer. The heavy smell of burnt clove rolled over Garrick when they stopped before him.

Garrick's captor stood.

"It is good to see you, again, Lord Karasacti," he said.

"Is this the one?" the man replied.

"It is."

The lord stepped forward, all three of his gray eyes scrutinizing Garrick. He was not as large as Garrick's captor but was obviously of similar species.

From this close the man's robe seemed to move of its own accord, shimmering with light, streaks of darkness floating in its weave. An invisible fist seemed to reach out from the robe as if to wrap its fingers around Garrick's heart, but it retreated before making contact, sliding back into the fabric as if it were pulled by the tides.

The man wrinkled his nose.

"He smells something awful."

"No worse than when I captured him, Lord."

The man grunted.

"Who are you?" Lord Karasacti asked Garrick.

"What does it matter?" Garrick replied.

The back of Karasacti's hand hit Garrick's jaw before he saw it. The power of the blow sent him crashing to the wall, chains rattling. The smell of cloves grew to a gagging force, and the movement of colors in the robe melded themselves into a single pattern that drew ire from the darkness inside Garrick.

"I asked you a question," the man said.

"Garrick," he muttered, checking for broken teeth. "My name is Garrick."

"This is a safe place to live, Garrick. Do you understand?"

"So far, I would argue with that claim."

He had just enough time to set his jaw before the next blow exploded inside his head and a bloody taste filled his mouth.

The odor of burning cloves intensified. He recognized it as the smell of the lord's magic, like the citric lemon of a Lectodinian's spell or the blood taint of a Koradictine's.

Different, though.

This man was neither Koraditine nor Lectodinian.

Garrick reached for his link but again found nothing. He sensed this mage before him, though. He felt his block and realized at the same time that Karasacti had also sensed his quest for a link.

The back of the mage's hand crashed against his head once again. Garrick's vision swam.

"Lord Karasacti!" the man who had captured him said.

The Lord whirled. "No one casts magic on this plane without my consent."

The hall grew quiet.

Karasacti turned back to Garrick, strolling the perimeter of his vision like a gladiator circling his opponent.

"How?" was all Garrick could manage.

"I own all the links," Karasacti said. His robe pulsed with color.

"This man's magic killed eight men, sir," the captor said. "I don't understand how he could do so without—"

Karasacti twisted his hand, and the words died wetly in the man's throat. "I said, *no one* casts magic on this plane without my consent." Karasacti dropped his hand and returned to face Garrick. The captor drew a deep, gasping breath as he receded into the background. "The punishment for unapproved use is quite specific."

The gathering pressed inward. Garrick could taste their interest.

Life force swirled within him.

He sensed constraint from Karasacti, felt boundaries that held lives in check. The man told the truth. This plane *was* safe, as long as the citizens played by his rule. But Garrick's dark energy felt more than that. He felt a young boy somewhere in their audience, watching with expectation, full of fear inside a tough outer shell—

would the lord discover his tryst with ReAnne, the love of his heart who had been promised to another? An older man steeled himself from reacting. His son had been killed for something Karasacti had claimed was a crime. A woman held her daughter in her arms. Another cradled a still unborn baby in her womb.

Garrick sensed it all, each piece falling into its place. Karasacti held the plans for each of them, and each of them would live according to his plans.

The force inside him wanted to reach out, wanted to fill each ache with its healing.

Why was he here?

Braxidane had placed him in this desolate plane and given him a sword that was a sure mark of magic, certain to draw the lord's attention. Had it been merely a beacon to call Karasacti to him? Did Braxidane intend for him to meet his doom here on this desolate plane?

The woman who escorted Karasacti gazed at Garrick, her brow knitting.

It was her unborn child Garrick felt.

Though she did not yet show it, the woman knew she carried the lord's babe. She was consumed with a bittersweet worry that the child be perfect and beautiful and free to live its own life, and she held a deep fear caused by the violent edge of Karasacti's demeanor.

Garrick's hand moved toward her, his fingers cupping themselves.

His chain clanked when his arm reached the length of its slack.

His life force pooled in his hand, feeling for her child. It was a girl, a strong girl. Garrick looked at her and smiled. This is why Braxidane had put him here. The child.

Garrick could feel her unborn god-touch already.

"It will be all right," he said to the woman.

All three of her eyes opened wider.

"Stop it!" Karasacti spread his arms and spoke a language Garrick had never heard. The aura of magic rose. The odor of cloves became cloying.

Garrick gathered the life force that remained inside him as Karasacti finished his chant.

"No!" The woman screamed as she raced toward Karasacti, magic of her own flickering its green fire between her fingers. It was not her magic she wielded, though. The source of her power lay instead in the child she carried.

She crashed into Karasacti, fouling the lord's spell.

He turned to her, rage etched in his cheeks.

"This man can help us," she whimpered.

Karasacti's spell was a black bolt that burned a tight hole high through the woman's chest, continuing through her and into the crowd, cutting men and women down everywhere it touched.

The woman fell to the floor, writhing in pain, two of her eyes clenched shut, the third wide with panic. "Help me," she moaned, turning that third eye to gaze at Garrick.

Garrick cast a bolt of what little life force he had left, but Karasacti brushed it away to explode in a shower of sparks against the far wall. Emptied, Garrick's hunger felt every soul in the marketplace.

The life forces of Karasacti's dead hung ghostlike in the air.

The lord's eyes blazed.

Garrick opened a link to the plane of magic and felt energy channel through him.

Garrick hated this man, he realized.

Karasacti was a wizard who bought and traded people without care, a man who pressed his will throughout a plane at any cost. Garrick had known men like this as he grew up, barons and dukes and men who ran businesses as if they were somehow above the common weal. It was this kind of man who had worn his mother down to the ragged woman she became. It was this kind of man who had left him unbound and drifting until Alistair had made him a home.

Garrick would destroy this man.

So resolved, he stood firmly, chained to the wall with his arms outstretched and his feet planted. He let go his restraint, and he called forth a frothing current built of every ounce of life force he had left in him, every scrap, every ort and speck and nit and pinch and peck until there was nothing left but vacuum, and then he found more. It poured from his fingertips in a single torrent, flowing toward Lord Karasacti in a brilliant burst of pure power.

Karasacti cast black flames at Garrick, and the two magics crashed like rams, exploding in a blinding flash that froze the room.

A scream filled the hall, and voices rose.

Then it was over.

Karasacti stood, panting with his exertion, his robe now disheveled and dirty, lined with grime, its pattern dull and languid. But he was alive and still strong.

He ran a hand over his brow and gave Garrick a smug smile of satisfaction.

"Is that all you have?"

Garrick hung limp and lifeless from his restraints, his life force expended, his head lolling forward, his eyes bloated and bloodshot. "No," Garrick said, bringing his hunger forward. "That is not all I have."

Disgust rose through the depths of his consciousness like a cold snake of mist and smoke. It was a dagger, a stiletto, a chilled, poisonous cloud of desire that Garrick let loose to wind its way through the hall, stretching, yearning, and wrapping itself around men and women, looping its foggy fingers around their necks and draining vapor into their mouths and through their noses and down, down, deep into the very beings of their lives.

A woman cursed.

A man screamed.

And, as Garrick breathed their energy in, he stood strong in his chains, pulling lives from their shells, grabbing power and funneling it into the limitless pit of his hunger. He pulled on his chains and ripped their cleats from their moorings, the shackles hanging from his wrists and ankles to clang on the rough stone floor as he strode forward.

Karasacti cowered now, his robe pulsing crimson in tandem with the rise of Garrick's hunger.

Garrick felt the robe as it fought to clamp his power, and suddenly he realized this robe was what gave Karasacti control of all magic across the plane.

"Who are you?" Karasacti said, holding his hand up against Garrick's progress.

"Braxidane placed me here."

"I should have known."

The robe flared with a prismatic river of colors that whirled as if they had been suddenly freed.

Garrick's hunger became a thing of its own then, drinking more lives and flowing their power into his being. Karasacti groaned, sensing his doom. Garrick nearly broke, then. He nearly pulled back to spare this man who may well have done nothing wrong beyond becoming corrupted by a power born for the sole purpose of corruption itself.

And he could have done it, too.

He had controlled this magic before.

But the voice of the woman came to him, whimpering. She was still alive. The baby inside her still grew. Garrick saw the charred hole glistening from high up in her chest and felt the need for justice stronger than he felt Karasacti's pain.

His hunger rose with self-righteous conviction. He reached out a hand, and Karasacti's body disintegrated into a pile of blackened mire, only his robe remaining behind, its folds lying in a pile of the dead man's ash. With a final breath, Garrick added the mage's life force to those that already filled him, then braced himself and brought his hunger into control.

He had succeeded.

Karasacti's magic was his.

Garrick watched the bedlam that reigned before him. Men and

women screamed and raced to get out of the hall. Powerful smells of magic mixed themselves into the sickening mass. The people here would revolt soon. They would learn Karasacti was dead, and then things would change in ways he could not predict.

His gaze finally took in the woman, lying on her back, her eyes wide, her breathing coming in panicked gasps. Her skin was clammy and slick with sweat.

"My baby," she whispered to no one. "My baby."

Life force roiled within him, and Garrick smiled.

"It's going to be all right," he said as he put his hand on her shoulder. "It's going to be all right."

CHAPTER
SEVENTEEN

The woman who had saved him was named Pru.

She loved words and she loved music. And poetry. She had been casting those forms of magic since she was a little girl and could conceive of no other life. All this Garrick gleaned from her more lucid ramblings as he followed her directions and carried her through Karasacti's castle, a monstrous construct of crystal, wood, and glass that towered into the purple nighttime sky.

They came to her chambers.

He laid her down on the bed and drained a thin stream of life force over her shoulder to heal her wound. He had no idea how well his ministrations would hold on this plane. The damage had been great, and her body needed time to recuperate, but her life force was strong around the tiny kernel of the child that grew within her.

Garrick took a seat in a recessed window where he could both watch her sleep and take in the prismatic colors of nightfall as it crossed Rastella. His body worked to process the foreign life force he had absorbed. It had a similarity to Adruin's energy but felt more caustic. More abrasive. The flow scrubbed his skin from the inside as if fighting to get out.

He looked upon the night.

The sky was purple and midnight blue, streaked with greenish-black clouds that were interlaced with intense pink and lavender. A pair of moons cast arcs of light across the buildings, creating a cross-hatch of shadows that seemed to shift and weave. The wind, which seemed to never stop on this plane, whipped with a strong force.

Dark figures gathered in the streets below, gazing upward and pointing to the suites where he and Pru were now sequestered. They yelled names and curses. They had been horrified as he strode through town with Pru's limp body in tow. He had seen their kinds of expressions before and had heard the questions they spat at him. To some, he was a demon. To others, an insane mage. To the rest he was he merely a bloodthirsty monster unleashed through some legendary force of darkness?

And just as he had heard each of these thoughts, he understood what would come next. They were afraid of him now, but it wouldn't be long before that fear turned to anger, and that anger turned to action.

How long did they have?

Minutes? Hours? Days?

His lack of certainty drove home the truth that Garrick did not know these people. Did not know this place.

The chamber they were in was large and well cared for. The bed was soft and padded.

A mirror covered one wall, reflecting Pru's image as she slept.

Despite her height, she was a slight woman. Her skin was soft and dark, olive with just a hint of purple. All three eyes were closed, and the cut of her jawline was smooth and relaxed. Her breathing was gentle.

Karasacti's robe hung on the hook where Garrick had thrown it. He took it to a basin to clean the dirt and grime from its weave. The fabric writhed in his hands. The cuffs of his shackles were still around his wrists and ankles. They clanked with dull retort as he scrubbed the material.

He felt the garment whisper to him.

Garrick wanted to wear it. The robe was how Karasacti had controlled the plane. He knew that now. If he put the robe on, it said, he would almost certainly be able to access his link and cast something that would remove the shackles. If he put this robe on, he might understand more about this plane and maybe even learn the magic it took to move through others.

Put it on, he thought.

Wear it.

But he had been around Braxidane often enough to be wary of such things and the prices they might carry. Actions and consequences, he thought. There was more here than he understood.

Instead, he worked at cleansing its fibers.

Soap lathered as he scrubbed.

Three times he washed, rinsed, and dumped fetid water.

Then he hung the robe to dry, dribbles pooling with a prismatic sheen on the dark floor below it.

He returned to the window beside the bed.

The crowd had grown as the night progressed. It twisted in the darkness like a black whirlpool of madness. Voices rose more firmly now. Oily fires burned from torches, and the people carried weapons that before were simple shovels and rakes. Karasacti was dead. The power on this plane had shifted.

They were coming.

The citizens of Rastella had enough of Karasacti's brand of magic and they were coming to take back their city.

He had to do something.

He looked to the bed where Pru lay, chest gently rising with her calm breathing. Green moonlight flowed over her. A lump grew in his throat. She reminded him so very much of Sunathri.

What was her role here?

The Lord's sorceress? His consort? His queen?

Would they bother her if Garrick were not here? She had, after all, been touched by Karasacti's magic. Would they trust her, or would they burn her like any other thing they saw as Karasacti's?

He scowled, realizing his selfishness.

Garrick was trying to convince himself to take Pru from her home, to kidnap her while she slept, merely because she had helped him and because she reminded him in some strange fashion of a woman he may once have loved. He should be better than this. Pru would be fine. This was a plane that understood sorcery. Still, he bent and placed a soft kiss on her forehead, then left her to sleep through the effects of her recovery.

A ceramic explosion came from outside the window, a bowl or decanter crashing against the stone wall. A throaty cheer rose. Another crash came, the sound of baked clay shattering. Then glass. A lower-level window was broken.

Garrick's life force swelled.

It would prefer to heal at this stage, but he had learned now how to make this power bend to his own needs. He could use it if he had to.

He looked out the window one last time and noticed a place down lower where a battlement rose to within leaping distance. If he could get there, he would be able to escape. But that meant he had to descend the tower. Without a second thought, he stepped out of Pru's bedchamber and ran to the central staircase, chains jangling from his wrists and ankles.

The entire castle was dark now. Paintings hung from the walls like pure black rectangles in a land of shadow that smelled of cloves.

He took the stairs down. His hand trailed over a banister that curled at the end of each flight, doubling back again and again to lead further downward. He slipped once, tumbling to the bottom of a well. Panting, he picked himself up and scrambled downward.

Voices echoed up the stairwell.

Footsteps caused Garrick to lean over the railing and see men coming forward. He took the doorway at the next floor, hoping he had descended far enough.

This room, too, was dark. The stench of sorcery hung here like a drape. Security wards, he thought. He had sensed them before. He ducked and rolled in an instinctive, workmanlike move that was made efficiently and without concern. His chains clattered against the floor as he rolled.

The blow aimed at his head missed.

The beast came from the shadows, black and purple. Eyes ringed its head, glistening with malignancy. It was a remnant of Karasacti's magic, a spell cast to protect something the mage wanted to be protected. The beast roared and pressed an attack.

Garrick cast a shield of life force over himself, and black talons met the cone with an explosion that scattered sparks of blue and red into the air. But the beast's magic penetrated his shield, and a sliver of cold steel froze Garrick's being.

He drew a breath, sliding himself backward.

He had to get out.

The stairwell was behind him. He slipped toward it, hoping Karasacti's magical beast was tied to the room rather than free to follow him. Voices boomed from a floor below. Torchlight illuminated the area with yellow-green shadows.

He was trapped.

The beast gave a pained roar as it stopped at the doorway. It was penned to the room—at least that much was in Garrick's favor.

"Holy Father!" a voice bellowed from below as the man in the front of the column saw the creature.

"The monster is creating more demons!" a woman's voice called.

Garrick climbed three stairs at a time.

The gang clamored from below. A tidepool of their need for vengeance swirled around them. A dagger whirled past, crashing against the wall before clattering to the floor.

He sprinted up the next flight.

"Come on," he heard a familiar voice above.

Pru stood at the lip of the stairwell. Her hair was disheveled from sleep, and she held her damaged arm at a tender angle.

As Garrick ran to her, she spoke words of magic.

Crimson fire flowed from her outstretched hand to form a barrier between Garrick and the people of Rastella. Confused voices filled the stairwell. He grabbed the dagger that lay at the top of the stairs, then came to her side.

"Thank you," he said.

"Cries of the townspeople woke me," she explained, still holding concentration on the spell. "You had best go."

"They'll vent their anger on you."

Pru smiled wearily. "It will be all right. I know the city. They'll shun me, but I don't want to be here, anyway."

Garrick nodded, seeing resolution on her face.

"There's no way out but down," he said.

"Use the lord's robe."

He hesitated. How could he tell her he didn't want to risk trifling with such powerful magics? How could he tell her about Braxidane?

A man pressed forward with his torch. Embers flared as the fire touched Pru's magic. Someone threw a weapon, and Pru's shield rebuffed it.

She looked at him, eyes glittering in shadow. "You had best go," she said. "I cannot hold this for much longer.

"All right," Garrick replied.

He put a light hand on her shoulder, then raced up the stairs.

The robe was where he left it.

He held it for a moment, turning the fabric over with his fingertips. It was still damp in the evening chill.

Voices came from below. Footsteps rumbled on the stairs.

With no time to waste, he slipped it on.

ALL OF EXISTENCE

EIGHTEEN

Garrick found himself in a place of nothingness.

There was no ground beneath his feet. No horizon. No sun, no moon, no wind, no land. There was only color and fragmented space, blobs of green, blue, red, and yellow formed shifting patterns like the view inside a kaleidoscope. His stomach lurched. He put his hand before his face and was pleased to gain some small sense of balance.

It seemed comfortable here, alive.

The robe he wore pulsed with color, molding around his skin.

He found the dagger still in one hand. Its plainness in this place of extreme queerness gave Garrick inordinate comfort. He wrapped his hand around its hilt and tried to stand more firmly.

As he focused, passages formed from nowhere, twisting this way and that, growing in hazy outlines at the periphery of his vision. The place was chaos formed of infinite structure—passages and more passages, an arcane maze of tunnels and shafts that shifted in an amorphous mass.

"Garrick," a voice said. "I didn't know if I would see you again."

"Braxidane," Garrick replied as he turned to face a formless blob of gray material.

"At your service."

"Unlikely."

His superior seemed to sit up, his edges folding over themselves as if they moved of their own volition.

"You've done well bringing the robe here," Braxidane said. "The planes are once again open to Rastella."

"What is this place?" Garrick said, feeling aimlessness.

"It is my home. We call it All of Existence. It's the place we live, the construct that connects the Thousand Worlds."

More colors churned, making Garrick sick to his stomach. His life force was quiet here, subdued and calm. He was comfortable. Yet still, Garrick looked at Braxidane and felt nothing but anger.

"You sent me to Rastella because of the child, didn't you?"

"Perhaps."

"I'm tired of playing your games," Garrick said. "Why am I here? When can I go home?"

"You still don't understand what I've given you?"

"You've given me nothing."

"I've given you the ability to change the course of the universe."

"Why would I want to do that?"

Braxidane turned the color of condescension.

"You've touched the child on Rastella, haven't you?" Garrick said. "It will grow up with this same curse I have."

"Yes, Garrick. Now you're seeing things like a true mage. The child will grow to be one of my champions, just as you are. Only it will not know any different life. For this woman, being god-touched will be all she ever knows."

"You've sunk to a new low, then."

"How so?"

"At least I had some form of a choice. The child is having this foisted upon it."

Braxidane's form shuddered with something Garrick interpreted as a shrug. "That is life, Garrick."

"No it's not," Garrick said, feeling his anger rise. "You singled me out because I was weak. But I'm tired of it. I'll not be your lap dog anymore. You can't just put me someplace, and expect me to jump."

"Down, boy," Braxidane said, his color deepening.

"Stop it!"

"Oh, grow up, Garrick."

Garrick turned away, wanting space between himself and Braxidane, but every path led to more paths and he could not determine the best way out. He picked one at random and strode toward it—or, rather, he flowed toward it.

Movement in All of Existence was different. It was ambulation via thought, more like swimming than the mindless motions of walking. As Garrick moved, the energy around him came to a boil, rushing, racing through him as if trying to crash into his body. The passage sizzled with invisible currents, swirling like storm winds against his skin.

He felt Braxidane behind him.

"It's all life force," Garrick said, realizing now why his hunger was so comfortable here. "Everything here is life force."

"I think of it as reality."

Braxidane hadn't followed him so much as appeared beside him.

"Stop with your overbearing gibberish."

"No, Garrick. It's your turn to stop."

Garrick sensed his superior's anger.

"Most people have to interpret life, Garrick. Most people do the best they can to understand the purpose of their existence. And most people limit themselves because they don't see how powerful they really are." Braxidane's form pulsed. "You, though—you've been given the privilege of seeing your essence for what it truly is. And you've been given the ability to use that essence to create something real."

"A lot of good it's done me."

"Only because you refuse to use it."

"Why should I steal energy from its rightful owner and funnel it into whatever strikes my whimsy?"

"What a quaint question, Garrick. What gives *me* the right to change the world? In the end, the only answer that matters is that you can."

"But I shouldn't."

"A purely subjective judgment, don't you think? And subjective judgments require a basis."

"Yes," Garrick snapped. "Actions and consequences. I get it."

He could sense Braxidane's childish grin.

"I suggest only that you use both your conscience *and* your intelligence to shape your concept of life."

Then he was gone.

It was a leaving done in a single, instantaneous moment. No flare. No scintillating cloud of glimmering color. Braxidane was just there one moment and gone the next, leaving Garrick alone in All of Existence.

Life force pulsed around him, pushing, moving between planes like water flowing from mountaintops. He steeped himself in it, feeling its motion, sensing its depth in the same way a sailor feels the ocean.

He thought about moving, and he did.

He thought about the planes, and the entrance to each of the Thousand Worlds was suddenly open to him, spread across All of Existence but easily within his reach. He felt the eternal, never-ending flow—life force in and life force out. He sensed connections and the nodes, and the eddy currents of calm like the location he had spoken to Braxidane in.

He chose a node with a random thought.

The robe pulsed, and Garrick found himself there.

It was a quiet place.

A calm place. A place with no pressure, no deadlines, no arguing mages, and no mobs of people banging down doors to get at him. He sat in this place for a long time, thinking, learning, feeling the heady flow of energy that wrapped around him, sensing the true nature of the worlds that comprised All of Existence. He didn't know how long he sat there. It could have been centuries, or it could have been a single heartbeat. It could have been a lifetime.

Did time even exist here?

Were the planewalkers, those beings that moved through this connective world, truly all-powerful?

Was he now a god?

NINETEEN

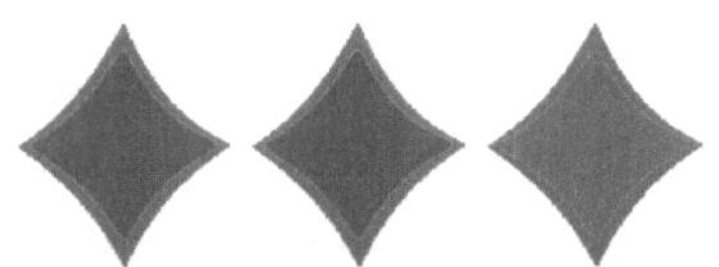

"Do you understand?" Braxidane said at last.

Garrick sat at an otherwise empty node, his "hands" spread into the flow, his eyes closed, his head thrown back, and his mind filled with pieces of lives he had never known. The robe pulsed an unending stream of color as it protected him from the flow. He smelled power. All of Existence—the planes, the connections, and the planewalkers—throbbed in his mind.

"You feed off energy," Garrick said.

"We feed off the flow," Braxidane said. "Energy in stasis has no purpose."

"Hezarin blocked Rastella's flow, so you had me fix it."

Braxidane's form grew a feeling of parental pride. "You're learning."

"If current is all important, why did Hezarin block the passage?"

"She was upset because I wouldn't alter the work you did to entangle the orders' god-touched mages. But when a god takes control of a plane, she owns the entire flow within it."

"Meaning only she can grow from it? Meaning others wither?"

"Yes."

Garrick thought about this.

"We once fought over planes for just that reason," Braxidane said. "Until finally it came to war throughout All of Existence."

"Starshower?" Garrick asked, dawning coming in the form of stories Darien had told him in the quiet nights when they had traveled together.

"Elsewhere it was known by other names."

Deeper understanding rolled over Garrick.

Storytellers made good coin telling of the cataclysmic event in Adruin's past that, until now, Garrick had viewed with healthy doses of skepticism and disdain. But he saw just how big the world was now. And now he saw how much like a spider's web it was, too, a sticky mass of choices and events that were all inextricably intertwined. The world was beautiful in its simplicity, awesome in its complexity. Garrick thought of the Shariaen ancients he had faced in the hills when he first traveled with Darien.

"War in Existence can happen again, can't it?"

"Some say it is happening already. Though our council of Joint Authority was another consequence of that first battle, it does not function as it once did."

"Why are you showing me this?"

"It seems to be the right time."

Garrick felt Braxidane's lie pulse through the flow. He moved his body and felt the robe surrounding him. It was the robe that had brought him here, the robe that had given him access to this place. Braxidane's story had given him nothing beyond confirmation of history he had already sensed. The planewalker loomed before him, shimmering silently with blue and green pulses. Was he hoping Garrick couldn't see through him? Was he still expecting Garrick to follow him like the puppet Braxidane was treating him as?

"There is much to think about," he said.

"Yes," Braxidane said. "But you have little time. You've got to go back to Adruin."

Garrick nodded.

Being here had changed him. It had given him sight into the minds of the planewalkers who controlled the flows of energy between the worlds. And being here had given him something else, too. Sitting in the flow, feeling the power these creatures wielded had taught him that the people of his plane—of any plane, for that matter—were subservient to the planewalkers in ways they could never see. They were puppets. Pawns. The planewalker's power was an invisible weight tied to every being in the plane. It meant that no one was truly free to live their lives, and having seen this truth meant that he, Garrick, was the least free of them all.

He thought of Pru's unborn child, already tied to her planewalker.

He could not let them win.

"I will lead your Torean House," Garrick said, feeling Braxidane's exhalation at the words.

"I thought your friend led the Freeborn."

"Darien is my friend, but he cannot succeed."

And at that moment, Garrick knew what he said was true.

Darien was familiar with people who wanted to be led, but Torean mages had no interest in organization. Their support at the outset had buoyed Darien's spirit, but he had been doomed to failure. Yet, leading the Freeborn was important to Darien. Wresting control from him would be devastating.

"I'll keep Darien with me," Garrick said. "It will work out."

"I don't care about Darien one way or the other," Braxidane said, flashing the color of a smile.

"So I will fulfill that part of my destiny. That's what you expect of me, do you not?"

"Of course," Garrick's Superior replied. "That has always been the natural consequence of your power."

Garrick paused at that.

The idea of being responsible for the mages scared him, but whether he deemed himself a worthy leader or not, the Freeborn would respond to him, and there was no one else on Adruin who could address the things that needed to be addressed. Actions and consequences. If the consequence of taking control of the Freeborn was that Adruin could be made free of the planewalkers, he was willing to take that action.

Braxidane's essence grew calm. The folds of his presence smoothed as trails of his being slipped into the stream around him.

"But one thing more," Garrick said.

"Yes?"

"I will lead your Torean House, but you have to agree to leave me be. No more pulling me back and forth. I'll do your bidding as best as I can. But I'll fight you if you whisk me away without warning again."

A row of cilia waved along Braxidane's farthest edge, stretching toward the flow.

"I'll hold you to your promise," Garrick said. "No meddling anywhere on Adruin."

Braxidane pulsed a lack of care. "I'll refrain from my *meddling* in your dealings if that's how it has to be—though you may find my distance troubling at some point."

Garrick grinned. "That is how it has to be."

Braxidane's coloring dropped brightness, the blues growing dull and the greens drab. He turned away and waved what might have been a hand.

"Go, then," Braxidane said.

And Garrick's vision swam.

TWENTY

Braxidane sat at his node, anticipating Hezarin's arrival.

It would not be long.

He dipped a tendril into the stream of consciousness that connected the Thousand Worlds, letting currents cross through him, feeling the balance that existed here. Cause and effect. Action and consequence. The flow had a simplistic beauty that he would never grow tired of admiring.

Hezarin did not disappoint.

He tasted the metallic nature of her approach, coming upon him fast, her shape pulsing with blue and red heat.

"You will pay for this, Braxidane."

"For what?"

"Don't play stupid with me. You sent Garrick to Rastella."

"And what if I did?"

"I had cordoned off that plane. Now anyone can get in there and—"

"Don't waste my time with false premises, Hezarin." Braxidane flashed with an acidic tone. "Rastella is a desolate plane. It has no value to you. You blocked it off only to spite me."

"The plane was mine, Braxidane."

"No. The plane was mine. You stole it and placed a dictatorial puppet on the emperor's throne, and then you gave him the robe so he could control the links."

Hezarin glared.

"You are, again, coming very close to violating every agreement we've ever made, Hezarin. That robe was one step too far."

"You're the one who sent a foreign mage into Rastella."

"Only after you opened the door and gave that mage the power of All Existence."

"Karasacti," Hezarin said with spite. "The man's name is Karasacti."

"I believe," Braxidane snapped back, "the correct tense is *was*. As in the man's name *was* Karasacti. It is not my fault that he was not powerful enough to handle the gift you gave him."

Hezarin emitted waves of animosity.

"Laugh while you can, Braxidane," she finally said.

Then she stepped back into the flow and was gone before Braxidane could reply.

He grumbled. An upset burn permeated the center of his being. Hezarin was right in that he had stretched the rules. Sending Garrick to Rastella was no more allowable than Hezarin's theft, but the fact that she had violated the agreements first wouldn't protect him from penalties in any formal inquiry. Leaving the sword with Garrick had been a particularly egregious breach of etiquette, though, and would not play well with Joint Authority—but she hadn't specifically mentioned the weapons, so perhaps he had gotten away with that small portion of his gambit. And at least Garrick had destroyed the robe. That would speak well for him.

Regardless, it had been worth it just to feel Hezarin's anger. Nothing was better than setting a radical on her edge.

He settled back and let tendrils drift into the flow.

With Hezarin on the warpath, he would have to be careful, but things were moving along nicely. Garrick's acceptance of his lot would help, and he had several other tricks at his command that might well cause his siblings in Existence to take note later rather than sooner.

Yes, he thought. It had been worth it just to feel Hezarin's anger, but he had plans.

Much bigger plans.

AFTERMATH

TWENTY-ONE

Darien, Reynard, and Ellesadil had just seen Ettril Dor-Entfar to his carriage.

The conference had gone as well as Darien could have conceived. The Koradictine leader had been open and direct, almost charming in admitting his order's errors, and he had promised to make things right with both the people of Dorfort and the Torean Freeborn.

Ellesadil, too, had seemed pleased with the conversation and had asked Darien and Reynard to join him for a post-session debrief. But now the clatter of anxious voices echoed from down the hallway. Darien couldn't make out the words, but it was obvious someone was excited.

"What's that racket?" he said.

"I don't know," Ellesadil replied with a grin. "But last time I heard such commotion, one of the chamber maids had just announced her engagement."

Footsteps pounded in the hallway around the corner. A girl from the stables appeared, her face flush and her hair flying in all directions.

"Please, Lord Ellesadil. Come quick."

"What's wrong, girl?" Ellesadil said calmly.

"It's Dane, sir. He's kilt someone. And Will's gone."

"Will?" Darien said.

"Yes, Lord. He's been stolen."

"Kidnapped?"

"Yes, sir."

A cold curtain of anger closed over Darien. "We've been duped," he said.

A darkness came over Ellesadil's face.

"Ettril should die for this, sir," Reynard said with cool firmness. "He set us up and fed us a line, and now he's stolen Will out from under our noses."

"Let's not jump to conclusions," Ellesadil said. He looked at the girl. "You said Dane killed someone?"

"Yes, sir, he did."

Despite her obvious effort to tell the story appropriately, the girl's words ran together.

"I was walking to the stable and I saw the body, and Dane laying all passed out, and all the blood. Just like I told Daventry, I don't know where he got the knife, but it was right there in his hand. Never seen it before."

Darien's heart clenched in his chest.

Reynard's face set as he glared at Darien. His glance burned with silent accusation. *Garrick wouldn't have let this happen*, that glare said.

Ellesadil held up his hand. "Slow down, young one. How about you just lead us to the stables and we'll see what we can find out."

"It's not your fault," Darien said, laying a hand on Daventry's shoulder and biting off his desire to yell at him.

The head cook sat on an overturned bucket used for bringing

water into the kitchen. His elbows were on his knees, and his head in his hands. He had just described his experience with Fil and his confusion at the odor coming from the privy.

"I should have said something. I knew something was wrong when I came from the privy, but I didn't say a thing."

"It's all right," Darien said.

"No it's not," Reynard said. "He *should* have said something."

Darien scowled at his councilman, and Reynard grew silent.

The kitchen crew stood about.

Daventry owned this room. He was constantly telling people what to do here, how to do it, and when it needed to be done. Now he was distraught. The crew stood in an informal row, staring slack-jawed, shuffling their feet, and generally wondering what was going to happen next.

"Come on, Reynard," Darien said, deciding to avoid the further discomfort of chastising his subordinate before the staff. "Let's join Ellesadil."

He let Reynard go first.

Reynard left in a huff, pulling his cloak over his shoulders to guard against the wind.

They found Ellesadil knelt over the dead body of a nearly bald man, maybe forty years old. He had been stabbed several times. A bloody stiletto lay in the dirt beside him. A younger boy sat on a bare stool against the wall, dabbing a wet cloth over his forehead.

A mare nickered from a stall, impatient to be fed.

"The boy doesn't know much," Ellesadil said. "He says he and Will walked into the stable, and the next thing he remembers is waking up beside this man with the knife in his hand and blood all over his shirt."

"This cannot be the work of a stable boy," Reynard said.

"I'm inclined to agree," Ellesadil said.

Darien knelt beside the lord and lifted one of the dead man's limp arms, bringing the fabric of his tunic to his nose.

"His clothes reek of Koradictine sorcery," Darien said. "Daventry reported he smelled the same scent before the kidnapping."

"What happened to the guard?" Reynard asked.

"They, too, apparently fell sleeping," Ellesadil replied.

"More improbable coincidence," Darien added.

Ellesadil nodded grimly.

"We've been made fools of," Reynard said. "Someone has to pay for this."

Darien stood. "We'll have time later to argue over what happened, who to punish, and how to prevent it in the future. But right now we've got to get the boy back."

"At least we finally agree on something," Reynard said.

"We'll need to discuss strategy."

"I've had enough of your strategy, Darien. We'll follow a course north because that's the fastest way back to de'Mayer Island."

"Their camp was to the west."

Reynard gave an exasperated sigh. "If they didn't head directly north, that means we'll get there ahead of them."

Ellesadil stepped between both men.

"You are in public, gentlemen."

Both members of the Freeborn glanced around. An audience of guardsmen, stable hands, and kitchen support stood like children caught stealing sweets.

"Take care of this man," Ellesadil said to the guards.

He turned back to Darien.

Darien's face burned crimson with embarrassment. He was tired of Reynard's constant friction. The mage fought him over every word of every policy. It would have to end. That was all there was to it. There were others of the house who could do the job. Amanda, in particular, had shown she could keep a calm head in difficult moments. When Garrick returned from wherever he had run off to, Darien would speak to him about a replacement but for now, Reynard was all he had to work with.

"Call your mages together and charter them to look for Will,"

Ellesadil said. "Since you're both right, I might suggest you split the Freeborn into two groups."

"That's a good idea," Darien said. "Call the Freeborn to my hall, Reynard. We'll meet in half an hour."

Reynard's glare could have set Darien on fire.

"I'll do that, Commander."

Ellesadil put one hand on each of their shoulders, and turned them toward the government center. He walked between them, pushing each along at a rapid clip. Once they were out of earshot, he glanced back and forth between them both.

"Another display like that and I'll see to it that the Torean house is removed from the city. Do you understand?"

"Yes, Lord," Darien said.

Reynard merely nodded.

TWENTY-TWO

Dressed in doeskin leggings and a tunic of Freeborn black, Darien stood before the gathering of the Torean mages. His battle helm from Dorfort's army was placed on the table squarely before him.

Reynard stood at his side.

Garrick, the Toreans' god-touched mage, had disappeared from before their eyes a week before, and now, earlier this morning, Will, Garrick's apprentice, had been kidnapped in an audacious gambit by the Koradictine order.

Clamoring voices made it feel like the air had been breathed out of the meeting hall. Every Freeborn mage in the city was here, nearly ninety in total. They were men and women who had come from various stations of life prior to taking up their sorcerous trades—fishermen, farmers, and woodsmen among others. A few were barely old enough to be out of their apprenticeships.

"What is the news of Garrick?" a voice called.

"Nothing new," Darien replied, knowing that answer wasn't good enough. Garrick's disappearance had happened in the very worst of circumstances, literally while he was addressing the Torean collective. The situation made him look weak, though even the lowest member of the House understood there was nothing to have been done for it. Not having progress was another thing, however. "We still have mages investigating his disappearance, and I have the guard scouring the countryside. But nothing is known at this moment."

The mages grumbled.

"Reynard and I agree, however, that we *can* still get Will back, so that's the course of action we will pursue. Reynard will lead a party to scour the north trails—the most direct path to the Koradictine homelands, and I will lead a group to the west where we know they last camped."

Reynard broke in.

"Those who wish to be in *my* party should come to this side of the room."

The hallway erupted in movement, every mage standing to move toward Reynard.

"Halt!" Darien called. He leaned over the table. "I said, *halt!*"

The Freeborn came to a grudging quiet.

Darien fought the urge to cast a foul glance at Reynard. How dare he stir them up at a time like this?

Earlier this afternoon, as he had walked into the chamber, he had been considering allowing the Freeborn to choose their assignments. It was a bolder move, a move a true leader might make to motivate people to greatness. One who chooses his task will rise above it, as his father once told him. But he saw now that this idea would have been a disaster. The entire troop had moved toward Reynard. The mage's expression was the clearest I-told-you-so Darien had ever seen. He was embarrassed and hurt, his dignity wounded.

After the room quieted, Darien spoke.

"Everyone on Reynard's side of the chamber will go with him. I will take the group directly before me. The rest will stay here and protect the city. I've asked Amanda to manage those who remain behind."

He motioned at the young woman to Reynard's left. Amanda smiled, but did not look happy. She had made it clear to Darien earlier that she would prefer to be out hunting Koradictines, and only his desperate plea that he needed someone he could trust to stay behind had kept her here. And, make no argument, Darien did need her here. Amanda had been at God's Tower. The mages knew her. She could keep them in order.

The gathering continued to grumble.

"I want to go north with Reynard." It was Trista, a youthful mage who was new to the Freeborn.

"We must use our resources in the most expedient fashion possible," Darien replied. "Don't you agree, Reynard?"

"Yes, Superior. We need to work together. We'll do as we're told, and we'll do it well."

The mages settled back in their seats, if not content, at least appeased.

Darien let go of a breath.

"That's it, then," Darien said. "Everyone is dismissed to prepare. We leave in an hour."

TWENTY-THREE

Darien wrapped his cloak over his shoulders and shivered in the chill of the overcast evening. The woods around his group smelled of a hard winter coming. The wind was a shiv against his exposed neck. It had taken them considerably longer to leave Dorfort than he expected, but once they were started they made good headway. Until, of course, it came time to scry.

Which they were doing now.

The mages were gathered in the clearing, using their wizardry to search for signs of Will or the Koradictines.

Watching them work together was the supreme test of Darien's patience. They talked in circles, covering the same points over and over in excruciating detail, arguing over fine points of finger positioning and the twists of vocal inflection and phrasing with such vehemence as to make even his teeth hurt. The day was growing short. And for all this work—ride an hour, dismount, cast spells, then do it again—they had gotten nowhere.

He should have just asked his father to send the Dorfort guard, who would have thundered directly down the path until they found the Koradictines.

Simple and direct.

Simple and direct, that is, if his father were well enough to be able to make such a command.

The downtime was what made the whole thing so excruciating. While the group moved he could keep his mind occupied, but as they stood here whiling away the daylight Darien had nothing to divert his thoughts from his father lying on his pallet, frail and failing of health. But he was the Torean commander, now. And among other burdens, this came with the need to do things at least partly their way. And that meant interminable waits while the mages tried their best to figure out what was happening.

He fiddled with the seam of his gloves, then shifted his sword for what had to be the tenth time.

"Are you finished yet?" he asked.

The wizards broke their spell.

"We are now," Carvil, a mage from the grasslands, replied.

"And?"

"Nothing, Superior."

Darien sighed. He heard the edge to Carvil's use of the word *Superior*.

"We'll try again next stop," he said.

Carvil didn't reply, but his expression was easy to read. *It would go better if you weren't hovering.*

What did they expect, though?

He was trying. Trying to bring the Freeborn into the world of the public, just as Sunathri had envisioned. They knew he wasn't a wizard when they accepted him for this post, but all he was getting for the effort were the insolent glares of kids barely out of their schooling. Surely, anyone could see how important it was to keep the Freeborn in Dorfort, that an order that held the confidence of the greatest power in the central section of the plane was an order to be dealt with.

He looked into the darkening sky and hoped Reynard's group was being more successful than his.

"All right," he said. "Mount up. We've got time for at least one more pass."

Reynard was certain that the Koradictines would travel north—as certain as he had been about anything—and he was the type who was certain about almost everything there was to be certain about. He was leading his team now, riding point through the pass. They had traveled most of the day, far enough they would need to make camp in the woods rather than return to the city. But they had found nothing. It was annoying, and watching his mages' enthusiasm wane as they realized they were in for a night out in the cold did not help anything.

He smirked, wondering if Darien's troupe was faring any better.

More than anything, Reynard wanted to be the one to bring Will back. It would be the last straw, the act that drew away the few stragglers of the Freeborn who remained loyal to Darien. The guardsman was a fine man at heart, but he was no mage, and, no matter what Garrick said, mages could not be led by someone without magic. If Reynard were the one who recovered Will, then even Darien would no longer be able to deny that the Freeborn wanted him to be their leader.

All afternoon Reynard had dwelled in daydreams of parading the Koradictines down Dorfort's streets. He imagined Ellesadil honoring him, Darien backing down, and the Toreans cheering.

Now it was growing dark and the rest of his troupe were as tired as he was.

Reynard brought his horse up in a clear meadow ringed by towering white birch trees, surveying the clearing as he waited for his mages to catch up. They could build a fire here in the leeward corner of the clearing where the trees would protect the blaze from the wind.

"We're not going to find a better place to stop," he said. "We'll camp here for the evening, and start fresh tomorrow."

Yes, tomorrow they could hunt again.

TWENTY-FOUR

Neuma sat quietly on the bench seat she had drug into Ettril's tent. The space inside the shelter was large enough to hold twice as many as the four of them, but suddenly seemed much smaller. For the first time since Ettril had accepted her plan, things were not going her way.

Yes, they had succeeded in taking the Torean god-touched's apprentice. The boy, Will, lay in a deep corner, incapacitated by Ettril's sorcery. But Garrick himself had not been there, and Quin Sar, the second-ranked mage of their order and a lifelong friend of High Superior Ettril Dor-Entfar, was now dead. Neuma had, of course, killed Quin Sar with her own hands and then made it appear as if a stable boy had surprised them. But none of the rest knew that, and she had no intention of letting them find out. The remaining Koradictines had gathered at the established point and made their way to this safe camp under the cloak of Ettril's spell work, which served to protect them from scrying eyes. No one could get near without him knowing.

Now, with things settled, the high superior wanted to know the truth.

"What happened to Quin Sar?" Ettril said, his crystalline blue eyes staring her down with birdlike intensity.

"I don't know how to explain it," Neuma said. She spoke the words exactly as she had practiced them throughout most of their hastily beat retreat. "The boy surprised us."

"You're telling me that one of the strongest wizards in the order was bested by a stable boy?"

"You've said yourself, sir: no matter how good the spell, a knife in the gut can spoil a perfectly good day."

"I don't believe it," Hirl-enat said.

"What *do* you believe?" Neuma snapped back. This was Ettril Dor-Entfar's interrogation, which was bad enough as it was. She wasn't about to let Hirl-enat make it any worse.

Hirl-enat glared at her.

Perhaps she could use his anger to her advantage.

"Go ahead and say it," Neuma said. "You think I killed Quin Sar myself, don't you? Go ahead and say it if that's what you think. At least then I can respect you for speaking your mind."

"I wouldn't be the only one who thought it."

"Enough!" Ettril said, his lips drawing into a tight line. He had been close to Quin Sar, and the loss was obviously difficult to bear. "I'll not have this argument now. Quin Sar is dead. And you can believe me when I say that I will get to the bottom of what happened, and that I will take whatever steps are required to deal with it."

Silence ensued.

Neuma finally spoke. "It seems we have a bigger problem to solve now, though, Superior."

Ettril Dor-Entfar nodded. "Yes, we do."

Hirl-enat stewed.

Fil, as usual, remained neutral.

"Where is Garrick?" Ettril said, staring at Neuma.

"I don't know any better than you do. I can't believe he wasn't there. Perhaps he's on an assignment? Did either Darien or Ellesadil have anything to say about him?"

"No, they did not. And they were each uncomfortable with my questions regarding him. I think his absence is as much a quandary to them as it is to us."

Neuma, happy the conversation had shifted, scratched at her cheekbone and thought about the problem. She had been counting on the Torean god-touched to remove Ettril from the picture—and Ettril to weaken Garrick enough that Neuma might best him by herself. Worst case, even if Ettril could not remove Garrick, the superior's fall, combined with Quin Sar's death would have left the superiorship open for the taking. But Garrick's absence had put that part of the plan in peril.

She nodded unconsciously. "Garrick will come as soon as he discovers the boy is gone. I'm sure of it."

"Don't we have an even more immediate issue?" Hirl-enat said.

"And that would be?" Ettril replied.

"The vigilantes from Dorfort are gathering. I suggest we need to exit these parts as soon as we can."

"I agree with that," Ettril said. "I cannot maintain this cover forever, nor can I keep the link isolating the boy going for much longer." The Koradictine superior had spent the past several weeks creating a holding chamber for their captive, linking it to himself such that any damage done to him would be equally performed on the boy. This, he felt, would pull Garrick's attention away and give him free rein to deal with the god-touched on his terms. But it was a difficult spell, requiring constant upkeep of the link. The effort slowed their progress.

"We'll have to do something else," Neuma said.

Ettril gave a grunt and nodded.

"We need to get rid of those who follow us," Fil added. "Sooner is better."

"I have a plan," Neuma said, glancing at Ettril and seeing an edge grow on his gaze. "That is, I have a plan, if anyone would care to hear it, of course."

TWENTY-FIVE

Braxidane must pay, Hezarin thought as she crashed through the currents of All Existence, flinging herself forward and letting energy scour her body as if it were a sandstorm. The flow burned through the sheerness of her span. It sizzled with a golden boil. She veered, barely noting the anomaly she would have run into had she not made a last moment adjustment.

It was a game she had played since the days when she was a newling. She loved the wildest streams, the ones that boiled and churned with their fury. She searched them out in the most remote zones of Existence, where she could be alone to enjoy the glorious *now* that grew from standing against the raw nature of life itself, letting it flow through her, getting caught in its eddies, its sinkholes, and its crashing rapids.

It was a dangerous game, but one that made her feel alive.

And today she needed to feel more alive than others.

Braxidane must die, she thought.

It was Braxidane's mage who had ruined her plans, and it was Braxidane who refused to do anything about it.

Yes, she thought, *Braxidane must surely pay.*

She stretched herself even more thinly, daring the current to split her if it could. Then she collapsed into a ball and let herself be carried into a temporary stasis lull. The flow of life force raced past, whispering in calls that rasped like a shower of boiling oil, a million voices that Hezarin let roll through her senses for just the briefest of moments.

"Damn them," she said. "Damn them all."

She leaped back into the flow.

Another anomaly slid past her.

A long passage loomed ahead, and she narrowed her profile, putting more energy into her run so she could build enough speed to shoot the gap. Sparks flared, and streaks of green and crimson wrapped around her, fading to dull turquoise. Electric fingers of neon broke over her skin as she careened through Existence.

Then she slowed, drawing herself into a protective orb and letting the current carry her away again until the rage subsided and she could hear herself think.

Finally, Hezarin breathed with a calmness to her sync. She was satisfied now. Content.

Her entire being tingled with exertion.

She flexed her outer shell and smiled at the thin edge of pain the movement brought her.

Refreshed and of a better mind, she flashed the color of a sigh and thought more clearly about Braxidane. Her brother had sent Garrick to Rastella, and Garrick had destroyed her hold on that plane. She should punish Braxidane for that directly, but as much as she enjoyed the prospect of that idea, as much as she yearned to see his expression fade as she ground him into the flow, Hezarin knew that Joint Authority would never let her destroy her brother.

A planewalker could live forever, and yet they had nothing of their own. They were, in effect, no more than vessels for life force—controllers at their best. Once the construct that made up a planewalker was gone, it was gone forever. Given this most reason-able justification, the council of Joint Authority tended to view simple trespasses against each other as acceptable, but killing another planewalker was the greatest crime she could commit.

Worse, her brother was a master politician, linked in a hundred places she knew of and probably a thousand more she didn't. Killing Braxidane would mean trouble in the best of times, and, given how the network was growing more sensitive each day, it could even lead to total war throughout All of Existence.

She flared the orange of deep thought and the aroma of a smile as she trailed a filament restfully behind, using it as a leisurely rudder as the flow carried her along. She couldn't kill Braxidane, but Garrick was another matter. Hezarin knew how to do it, too. Ettril Dor-Entfar, the High Superior of a sect of mages who flew her banner on Garrick's plane, had reported that Braxidane's god-touched had a weakness, a connection to a stable boy that Garrick had saved from a droll life.

She could use the boy.

And she could use Ettril Dor-Entfar, too. The mage had been smug as he reported that he had kidnapped the boy, as if his previous failures could be washed away with this single act of cunning.

Hezarin rolled into her node and relaxed.

She reached a thin rivulet of red out through the multiple layers of Existence until she touched the gateway to Adruin. Braxidane had braced the entryway, but—as she had expected—had not felt confi-dent enough to completely block it.

She would make him pay for that weakness.

A moment later, she had wrapped mage work around the life force of Ettril Dor-Entfar, pleased to find the sorcerer's essence already tied to the stable boy's. Perhaps the mage truly was was a cut above the rest.

When she was done, she retreated to her node.

She found herself dancing and singing to herself as she hashed out her plans. She couldn't wait to see Braxidane's anger. Just the thought of his expression made her feel better now than she had in a long while.

When she was ready, she flared with crimson power, lifted Braxidane's barrier, and slipped into the plane.

She had a debt to call, and there was no time to waste.

TWENTY-SIX

Ettril Dor-Entfar planted his walking staff into the soft ground of the hillside and hauled himself up another step. The plan to attack the Freeborn called for surprise, and that meant leaving the horses behind and climbing to his position on foot. So now his legs felt like putty and his hand was cramping around the staff so badly that it felt as twisted as the wood itself.

The night was overcast, which was good for tactics but made him anxious. As much as he wanted to ignore the fact that he was getting old, his eyesight just wasn't as good as it once was and the bitter wind had a damp aspect that hurt his lungs in ways he was sure he had once been able to ignore. His only blessing was the blanket of silence he had cast earlier, a magic that swallowed the rustling of his footsteps and allowed him to grunt, groan, and otherwise complain as he picked his way up the wooded hill.

The other roles required even more physical activity, though. Otherwise, he would have wondered if Neuma was trying to cause his heart to go bad.

The woman was dangerous, but she was also brilliant.

A terrifying combination.

He held onto the front of his robe and climbed the last steps to the ridge.

The Freeborn camped in the depression below.

He cast a brief spell to sense where everyone was and found ten Torean mages, and, of course, their citizen leader. One man was on guard. Ettril could also sense Fil, Hirl-enat, and Neuma as well as the lower mages who had accompanied them, each in their proper places. He smiled, enjoying the essence of a well-made plan.

Seeing everything was in place, he set gates and reached into the plane of magic. He let the flow trickle at first, chanting in a low whisper. Magic collected about him in tendrils of darkness that rose from the dead leaves. As they thickened, his voice became a steady hum. Soon the night grew so dense he could no longer see the sleeping Freeborn.

He smiled and lowered his voice.

His work was finished.

Now it was up to the rest.

It had been a very long day, and the nighttime didn't promise to be any more comfortable.

Darien was tired.

The mages were testy and hungry.

By the time he set the guard rotation the sky was dark and the wind had become a biting wail. He retired to his bedroll and built a small fire of his own. As he ate his cold dinner he thought of Garrick and Sunathri, and of how the three of them had met for the first time in a clearing of wood not much different from this one. Life is full of twists and turns.

Was this what he wanted? To lead people who despised him?

Who did he have to call his own now?

No one, he realized. Both Garrick and Sunathri were gone. He had only himself and his father, who was ill and fading even as Darien sat here in the cold woods. He settled into his bedroll, feeling deeply alone and wondering if he would be able to sleep at all. But the events of the day had worn on him. He drifted off almost as soon as he lay down.

DARIEN RACED ON HIS HORSE, sword blazing in the sun.

His warriors hacked at the Koradictine line. Sorcery and thick wood smoke swirled overhead in maddening clouds. Men grunted, women screamed, and mages spoke spells.

The enemy was a sea of battleaxes that gleamed like black death, blades flashing as men died. Still, he rode his charger forward. He was cut. Blood ran down his leg. For every opponent he destroyed, two more took their place, and, still, the Koradictine army pressed ever onward, voices rising in triumph. He was drowning, drowning in a sea he could no longer deal with.

"Retreat!" he commanded, raising his sword.

"Retreat!"

DARIEN SAT BOLT UPRIGHT, waking to the bloody smell of Koradictine magic he had grown to know too well. Darkness cloaked the camp, but he could never mistake that odor. He had smelled the reek of it in the depths of Arderveer and again on the battlefields of God's Tower.

Footsteps came from the forest.

Jason, his primary guard, groaned: "What? Arh—"

Darien's fire had faded to embers, but his sword was there, glinting reddish with its magical glimmer. He grasped the weapon and stood fully as he peered sharply into darkness so thick that even light from the blade could not cut it.

The sound of breaking branches came from somewhere outside the ring of camp.

The odor of curdled blood grew stifling.

"Wake up," Darien called, but his voice seemed dull and dead. He found the man beside him. "Carvil?" he said, pushing the mage's shoulder with his foot as he peered more deeply into inky darkness.

Carvil stirred and then, seeing Darien's drawn sword, snapped awake.

"Wake up!" Darien yelled this time. "Koradictines! Wake up!"

Incarnadine magic came from three points around the perimeter. A blast caught Ragan as he stood. The Torean fell heavily and did not move again.

Carvil spoke halting magic.

Darien gripped his blade tightly and raced toward the place where the spell work had originated. The ground was freezing against his bare feet, but he ignored the cold as he fought the magical mire of blackness that wrapped itself around him. He lurched forward, but it was like wading through a swamp. He hacked at the nighttime and felt the mire loosen. A moment later it flowed back, however, and he was again fighting the muck.

A mage stood behind a row of thorn bushes, casting.

Darien leaped over the brush and swung his blade. The mage cast a bolt of energy that burned like acid as it caught him on the thigh. Darien screamed and pulled his leg back, but his blade found its full purchase and split the Koradictine nearly in two.

Sorcery lit the area with yellow and orange strobes.

Darien saw the full story in those flares.

Koradictines ringed the area, casting in alternating volleys, cutting down Torean mages as they slept or as they emerged from their bedrolls. The forest lit up in flames, and a Torean screamed from somewhere.

Darien ran to the next sorcerer. He raised his weapon high,

catching the mage in mid-spell. Without waiting for the mage to fall, Darien continued, his mind lost in the battle. Pain stabbed his leg at each step, and his feet were now numb. Footsteps crashed through the forest from all directions at once. His blade found another mage, and he raced on.

Time passed without passing until he realized the only sounds around him were those of his own rushing about, of sticks breaking under his cold feet, and of his blade hacking to clear brush from his path.

He stopped and listened.

The air smelled of ammonia, carbon, and burnt wood.

Men lay on the ground.

He went to the first. Logan. His chest was burned nearly through. His eyes bulged in a dead stare. Next was Trentor, who lay face-down on the ground near the embers of their fire. He had lost an arm and lay in a pool of liquid darkness that gleamed slick and crimson. Darien rolled him over and saw that Trentor, too, was dead.

True panic came to him, then.

His glance flittered over the clearing, its trees merging with shadowed darkness, unable to stop in any one place. A chill that had nothing to do with the cold crossed his spine. His toes ached in sudden proximity to the fire, and pain scrubbed his thigh.

A faint voice moaned.

Carvil.

Darien hobbled to his side.

The man's stomach glistened with blood in the darkness, but he was alive. Barely.

"Come on," Darien said. "Let me draw you nearer the fire."

"Don't touch me," Carvil muttered. His breathing was shallow.

"I've got to get you warmed."

Carvil swallowed, then looked at Darien with accusing eyes. "I hope ... you're satisfied." He closed his eyes.

With that, the last Torean wizard in Darien's party died.

TWENTY-SEVEN

"That was fine work, Ettril," a voice came from nearby.

Ettril's heart jumped, but he was too tired to react. Instead, he slowly turned to find a large porcupine with pins as long as daggers staring at him. It had glistening black eyes. Heat rolled off its body in waves that, for just an instant, made Ettril want to warm his hands in it.

"Who are you?" Ettril said.

He regained his wits and clenched his hands around his staff.

"Don't bother with your magic, wizard. We've met before. I'm concerned you don't recall me."

Ettril peered at the creature and this time did manage to see a familiarity in the way the porcupine's gaze glittered. He sensed, also, the aroma of power that now seemed so ingrained in her aura that he couldn't understand why he hadn't felt it before.

"Hezarin," he said, giving a shallow nod of the head as his bow. "It is good to see you again, Milady."

"We can do without the pleasantries. Given the way you botched the entire exercise with Jormar, I'm almost certain you do not think it is good to see me again."

"Surely you can see Jormar's loss was not my fault," Ettril said. "The *Lectodinian* god-touched caused our problems, and the Torean mage was lucky."

Hezarin's quills ruffled. Her eyes drew to beads, and a fire's heat rose from her belly. "There is no such thing as luck, Ettril. Only deeds. You failed to deliver your end. Your order has lost my god-touched on this plane. *You* are the lord superior here, are you not?"

He took a firmer position with his feet and squared his shoulders. No matter how tired he was, he would not take this kind of abuse like a mouse.

"That I am," he said. "What can I do to repair this failure?"

The porcupine smiled. "That's better," she said. "I have need of you elsewhere."

"Then I will go."

"Exactly," she said.

Magic rose then. Ettril's mind twisted and his feet lifted, or perhaps it was the ground that folded itself and fell away. He could not tell. But when his trip was complete, the high superior of the Koradictine order was no longer standing and no longer in the woods.

He was, in fact, no longer on the plane of Adruin.

LECTODINIAN UPRISING

TWENTY-EIGHT

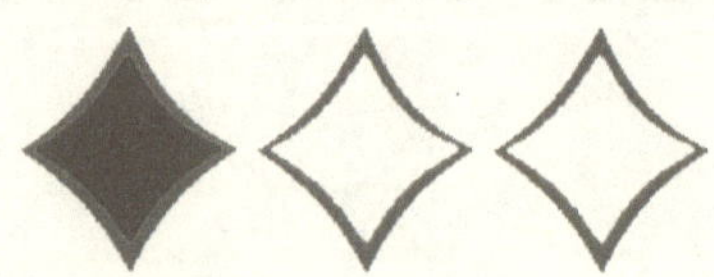

It was early morning, and a crisp wind blew against the closed shutters of Zutrian Esta's laboratory, sending a ruddery rattle through the chamber. Winter was coming early to the mountains this year. The leaves had already turned, their edges grown russet and crimson in the red rays of the sun, their bodies curling inward as they fell to the ground. The window sills gave a staccato rattle, drawing Zutrian's concentration from an elixir that bubbled with green froth.

Zutrian grumbled.

Being the high superior of the Lectodinian order meant there was never enough time. He had woken early in an attempt to enjoy the craft of his spell work, but he was having difficulty concentrating and his elixir was bubbling too strongly.

The window rattled again.

Salt.

He needed salt to control the process.

Zutrian went to a row of shelves and slid a glass pane back. He remembered a time when his mother would stand over the cooking pot, sipping from the ladle and deciding whether to add sage, cinnamon, or whatever bit of magic she thought would make the broth interesting. She would have made a good mage, he thought as he returned to the potion.

He dribbled a pinch into the mixture.

The potion calmed into a translucent emerald soup.

Zutrian nodded absently and opened his link to the plane of magic, letting the proper portion of magestuff seep into the mixture. A sliver of blue appeared in the cup, then dissolved into the base.

Yes.

Potion magic was like watching a grandchild, he thought. He never got to do it enough.

A pounding came from the door.

Zutrian scowled and straightened. "Enter," he said.

Arasia, a chambermaid, entered with a tray. She was young. Her hair was tied in a utilitarian bun at the back of her neck. "Your breakfast, Superior."

A man loomed behind her like a buzzard in the doorway.

"The sun isn't even up, yet," he said to Halsten.

"What, sir?" the maid replied.

"I'm sorry, Arasia, I wasn't speaking to you. Thank you for bringing me breakfast."

"You're quite welcome, sir. You've got to eat better."

"I'll try."

The chambermaid put the tray down at his table. As she left, Halsten slipped into the room. The echo of his boots on the flagstone seemed to ring in the day.

Zutrian pulled back the corner of the linen covering his food. The aroma of apple-scented oats made his stomach come alive. He cupped the bowl in one hand, letting heat seep into his fingers as he took a seat on the hard-backed chair that was upholstered in the earthy style of Badwall's western culture.

"I need your council, Superior," Halsten said.

"I assumed as much."

"Your edict that we remain undetected is causing problems."

"Hmmm?" Zutrian spooned his first bite of breakfast.

Halsten drew near, wrapping his hand over the back of another chair, hesitating as if waiting for the superior to add something.

Zutrian merely chewed and beckoned him to continue.

"There is a village to the north, sir. Jayalla, I think it's called. If we run the training exercises I have planned, then the village will certainly be alerted to our presence."

"So, what do you recommend?"

"I suggest a nighttime raid, sir. Something quick, that removes the village from the map in total."

"I see," Zutrian said. He scooped another bite of his cereal but left it in his spoon. "And what do we do with the people?"

"I'm sure we can sell them to Rickard."

"Rickard is in the farthest northlands."

"True."

"Winter is coming. Do you want to trek an entire village through the northlands in ice and snow?"

"I think we could do this quickly enough to avoid weather."

Avoid weather, certainly, Zutrian thought. At least the mages could. Displacing an entire village in the winter months would, however, result in more deaths during the ensuing march than occurred in the raid itself.

"And how do you suggest we handle the scouts and rangers?"

"Superior?"

"The scouts and rangers, Halsten." Zutrian's temper rose despite himself. His stomach knotted as he left the cereal to cool on a low table. "I didn't choose this place as our stronghold by accident, you know? I know this land. I know its people. I know how it smells and how it tastes. If we wipe an entire village from the face of the plane, the land will attack back. Rangers will note its disappearance, and they will talk. Stories will pass through towns and seep throughout the plane as sure as vines grow in the forest."

"If that's true, why *did* you choose this place?"

"Because the order needs its space, Halsten. We are still strong, but the loss at God's Tower has shaken our confidence. We need to regroup and build the right skills to finish the job before us. Vapor Peaks is secluded enough that we don't need to overrun anyone to do that."

There were other reasons, too, of course—reasons Halsten had no need to know of. Zutrian had made a mistake by trusting the Koradictines and it had cost a resounding defeat at God's Tower. So now he brought the order together in the Vapor Peaks, the land where he had grown up, a land he had spent years exploring, and a land he had once known so well he could determine his location by the mere slope of a hill or the gurgle of a creek full of clear springtime water.

The Vapor Peaks were central to the plane, a prime place to control the actions he would take in the first wave of his *new* plan. It was a place where he could oversee the destruction of the Koradictine order and a place from where he could then spread in any direction that made sense.

And it would all happen in the springtime.

But he held these plans close to his vest now because he knew that shared secrets always found ways to slip out of even the most tightly locked boxes. He had no interest in having them discovered.

"The village is in the way of my plan," Halsten said.

"Then create another plan."

"The northern face is perfect for our exercise. It's open and easily observed from even the lower peaks. I can post my camp there, and watch each of our mages as they work together."

"There is land to the south."

"It won't be as useful."

Zutrian's voice grew brittle and his gaze became a single pinpoint. "But it will serve. And, it supports our overall mission better."

Halsten dropped his gaze to the floor, nodding. "I'll get you a new plan, Superior."

"Good."

The mage turned, his shoulders rounded in defeat.

"Halsten?"

"Yes, Lord Superior?"

"You were right to bring this to my attention."

"Thank you."

Halsten stepped out. The door swung closed behind him.

Zutrian rubbed his eyes. The lack of sleep affected him more now than it had just a few years prior. The green elixir sat on the table across the room. He needed to spend more time casting, he knew, if only so he could feel comfortable calling himself a wizard.

He collected his bowl of oatmeal. It was cold and pasty now, but it still filled his stomach.

Another knock came to his door.

"Come," he said.

It was Batar, responsible for all the supplies the camp required, be they foodstuff, mage tools, or anything else.

"I need you downstairs, Superior."

"Can it wait?"

"No, Lord. It's important."

Zutrian glanced at his breakfast. His stomach grumbled. Standing, he spooned a last mouthful and left the bowl for Arasia to handle.

Two days later, Zutrian sat on his open porch wearing only a pair of linen trousers and a woolen poncho draped over his shoulders. The morning sun was brilliant against the cold bite of the mountain air. The stone was warm against his tailbone and the back of his crossed legs, though, a remnant of his recent spell work.

"Superior," a voice came from behind him.

It was Halsten, of course.

The mage shifted uncomfortably.

"What is it," he said, not turning from his meditation.

"I wanted your approval to release the first Koradictine raid."

A spike of anger shattered Zutrian's calm and destroyed his magic. He turned to the man, stood, and suddenly experienced the sharp pain of the balcony's true temperature as a blast of cold mountain air struck him full in the chest..

"I ordered that party to leave last night."

His lieutenant started to say something, then stopped.

"Did I, or did I not, meet with you and the rest of the commanders until the moon had fallen last night?"

"Yes, Superior. You did."

"And was I, or was I not, clear about my expectation that the operation against the Koradictines should commence?"

Halsten's lips drew to a straight line.

"So, tell me again why you felt the need to interrupt one of the few moments I have to myself?"

"I'm sorry, Superior."

"If you're trying to gain my notice, you'll find there are better ways."

"Yes, Superior."

Zutrian strode into his chamber where a fire's heat greeted him. Halsten was like most of his commanders. They were all power-hungry, anymore. Maybe it was because he was getting older—nowhere near "old," of course, but older. Discussions were sure to be happening, rumors and petty little struggles inside the order as members jockeyed for position underneath him.

Let them struggle.

He had no plans to leave this post for a very long time.

Halsten's footsteps noted his return from the balcony. The door shut.

"Make the operation happen, Halsten. I want the Koradictines completely hamstrung on this side of the plane throughout the winter months. Report again in a week."

"Yes, Lord," the commander said, bowing, and then leaving Zutrian's chamber.

Zutrian Esta removed the poncho and rubbed his arms before the fire. He was more tired than he could ever remember. But it would pay off. He had the entirety of his Lectodinian order housed in the Vapor Peaks, now.

One by one he would pick off the Koradictines.

By the springtime, they would all be gone.

That would leave only Garrick and his rag-tag Torean order.

For them, he had other plans.

TWENTY-NINE

Halsten led his team of five Lectodinian mages through a wooded glen. He was anxious, but certainly pleased to be doing something, even if it was just a simple precursory cleansing. A dusting of snow lay on the ground, and the horses' breath billowed with each exhale. The morning sun hugged the horizon behind them. The smell of a wood fire came from ahead. A house built of log, mortared with clay and soil, stood nestled into the hillside across the shallow gully. It was a sleepy house, he thought. Poorly built. Appropriate for a Koradictine. Served the mage inside right.

He raised a gloved hand to bring his mages to a halt, then turned to Marcus, his second, and motioned him to go around the far end of the property.

Marcus's head was wrapped in a heavy scarf that revealed only his brown eyes. He nodded and turned his horse to the north. Trae and Martin went with him. They had been over the plan in detail late into the evening last night, sitting in Halsten's tent and drinking tea warmed over an open fire. Halsten wouldn't mind a bit of that fire right now. He rubbed his hands together, then stopped when he realized the motion created an unnatural noise.

No excuses.

He had reminded everyone of that fact as they prepared to break camp.

No excuses for failure.

By the time they returned to the Vapor Peaks, the Koradictine order would lie as dead in this region of the map as if it were a physical body, a Lectodinian stake jutting from its chest. And he would own a part of that stake.

That should be enough to draw Helena's attention. He was sure she would be his once she saw what he was prepared to become. Waiting, and sitting silently on his mount, he thought of regaling Helena with the tale of the exercise. It would be warm there, wherever they were. They would share a mug of spiced ale, and Helena would gaze at him with those green eyes of hers that could make a man shudder from across the room.

He smiled at the image, despite a blast of cold air that made his teeth hurt.

A film of frost clung to a brown vine of ivy at the bottom of an elm. The morning bit at his lips. His ears hurt despite being tucked into a cap under his woolen hood.

No Koradictine was worth losing part of an ear to frostbite.

He pressed against the hood to make sure they were still covered.

They would wait here until Marcus was ready, then descend upon the log cabin silently.

Xavi-dar, the Koradictine, was inside.

Their order knew Xavi-dar from the magewar. She had come to this ranger's cabin after the order scattered, apparently having been injured. The ranger had taken her in—no surprise there. Xavi-dar needed no elixirs or love totems to attract a mate.

Halsten couldn't help fantasizing for a moment on what condition she might be in when they sprang their trap.

She was smart, though. Sharp and quick of wit. Her magic was strong if she was given time to collect herself, but took a long time in its concoction. If they could surprise her he had no doubt of the outcome.

An owl's call came from the other side of the glen.

He counted.

At five the call came again.

He clicked his tongue twice, pointing Regith and Forsyth to their positions. Halsten, himself, took the middle path, pulling on his link to the plane of magic and casting his spell before him. His wizardry met with that of the others. A shimmering blue net drew down over the house as they advanced.

Closer, he said to himself. *Closer*. He held the magics of each mage together. If he let them go too soon, Xavi-dar could wriggle away.

He guided his horse onward, holding the spell firm. The animal nickered and pulled his head to the left, but Halsten brought him under control.

They came to the rolling hill at the foot of the house, emerged from the woods, and rode past a work shed that was lined with a pile of freshly cut kindling. The net drew tighter as the ring of mages closed on the house. The smell of Lectodinian magic covered the ground like a morning mist.

There was a fire in the hearth. Halsten felt it against his chest. He felt the warmth of two bodies sleeping, too.

One stirred suddenly and moved about.

The net gave a cobalt glow as the mages poured more energy into it.

A muffled voice echoed from inside the building.

The door flew open. Xavi-dar held a robe about her. She was chanting and pulling what energy she could from her link, but it was too late.

Halsten dropped the net and felt the fire go out inside the house. Crystals formed in mid-air. Xavi-dar froze in mid-sentence, her spellwork dying on her lips.

ANSEL SLIPPED SILENTLY into the booth next to Yaragath, a man who had certainly seen better times. It was a move he knew well, a move he had done many times before though he was still quite a young man, an elementary motion for a lithesome mage who was used to living at the edge of shadow. The moon had been up for hours, and a cold wind blew outside the tavern. A candle of fatty paraffin burned with black smoke at the center of the rough-hewn table. A still smoldering pipe lay sideways against the tray the other man was using to catch ash.

"What do you want?" the man said, hunched over a ceramic mug. His voice was coarse and phlegmy.

The Koradictine was even older than he looked. The man's skin was soft and yellowed. He smelled of drink. His eyes were veined with crimson, and his wolf skin coat smelled like it hadn't been washed since before it came off the animal.

"I wanted to say hello," Ansel said.

Under the table, he slipped a dagger from its sheath. The blade was balanced to perfection for his hand. He closed his fingers expertly around the grip.

Ansel had been following Yaragath for the past several weeks, tailing him through Whitestone and watching the mage fall into the depths of depression the likes of which he couldn't understand. He had been separated from his order, certainly. And Toreans had chased him unmercifully for months afterward.

But he still had his magic.

And that meant he was still dangerous.

Which was why Ansel was sitting here in one of the darkest corners of a rot-gut tavern outside Whitestone.

"Who the hells are you?" Yaragath said.

"A messenger."

The older man laid his head back and peered at him through his drunken haze. "From who?"

"Why do you drink so much, old man?"

"I see," Yaragath grumbled, then lifted his mug to his lips. "My wife sent you." His chuckle was brief.

Ansel was nonplussed.

He was an assassin, a job that never bothered him because he figured they all deserved to die somehow. He didn't mind the idea of killing a defenseless man. He was a professional, after all. He spent days or weeks or months arranging his jobs and specifically setting up circumstances to leave him with no exposure. In that light, killing a defenseless man was the entire idea.

But, in the quiet times, Ansel described himself as a messenger of judgment, a man who carried out tasks that must be done.

Killing a man was meant to be a punishment.

Yaragath was Koradictine, and should pay for his transgression against the order.

But this man was a hollow shell—he had given up, he had nothing left worth taking in extractment of the justice that Ansel needed to feel good about his chore. Yaragath seemed to have already punished himself, and, to the best of his knowledge, Yaragath had no wife.

The idea annoyed him to the point that he now found it difficult to arrange his mind in such a fashion as he could kill the old man.

"I'm serious," he said.

"What?" Yaragath replied.

He had probably forgotten Ansel was there.

"I asked why you drink so much."

Yaragath gave a throaty laugh. "How old are you?" he finally mumbled.

"Old enough," Ansel replied.

"Hmm."

"I've been on my own since I was eight."

"Good for you, son. Good for you."

The old man's tone raised a hackle along Ansel's spine, but he didn't say anything.

Yaragath gazed intently toward Ansel. "You never lost no one, have you?"

"What do you mean?"

"Kids. Parents. Hell, friends for that matter. You've been alone since you was …," he looked at Ansel with a pleading question.

"Eight."

"Eight. Right. I seen boys like that … bet you never had a friend your whole life."

Yaragath reached for his pipe, missed once, then scrabbled his fingers along the wood to get hold of it. He put the stem in his mouth and pulled, releasing smoke from his nose.

"Who did you lose?" Ansel asked, uncomfortable being under Yaragath's analysis.

The Koradictine's eyes grew unfocused again. "I had a boy."

"What happened?"

"Magewar."

"Was he Koradictine, too?"

Yaragath started, and peered at Ansel. "Did I say I was Koradictine?"

"Sure," he lied. "You told me about how you made it all the way from apprentice to commander."

The old man grunted.

Ansel sat quietly.

"I shoulda paid more attention."

"What happened," he said. "To your boy."

"Lectodinian cut him down before he could get his spell away."

"Hmm," Ansel grunted.

"I told him!" Yaragath said, slamming his hand against the table. "I told him, again, and again. Speed. A mage in battle has ta cast quickly. He wouldn't lissen, though. My fault. I shoulda taught him better."

The dagger felt heavy in Ansel's hand. He wasn't sure he could do this.

"But I got 'im back," Yaragath's eyes glittered conspiratorially.

"How?" he asked, hope rising.

Yaragath leaned into Ansel's ear and gave a yeasty whisper.

"I followed the Lectodinians and picked them off one-by-one." The old Koradictine's eyes glimmered. He grinned, almost as if he knew it was what this lithe stranger needed to hear.

"One-by-one," he chuckled. "Very slowly."

The blade slipped between the mage's third and fourth ribs, slicing upward to find his heart.

Yaragath's body shuddered. A question came to his expression— followed by a sarcastic grin. "Maybe you did come from my wife," he said as he slumped against the wall, his pipe falling to the table again.

Ansel withdrew the blade and slid from the bench to walk into the wintry night.

He had a report to make, and he wanted to be long gone before anyone noticed the pool of blood that would soon spread over the tavern's dirt floor.

CARA HAD BEEN CLIMBING all morning.

She was tired and she was cold.

She didn't have anyone to blame but herself, though. She had, after all, volunteered specifically for this mission on purpose. But who would have thought that a Koradictine wizard would choose to live in the bleakest mountains north of Victory Fields, a piece of ground where no mammal could exist without a layer of blubber a hand's width thick and where even the simple act of removing your gloves to strike a fire threatened frostbite?

This went a long way toward explaining Yorl Maggore and his eerie idiosyncrasies.

Below her, the mountain fell sharply into open space that seemed to have no bottom. The air was sharp and biting, burning her nose and searing her lungs with each intake. Her legs ached, and her arms felt like they could fall off any moment.

She reached up and grabbed a ledge. She used her pick to leverage herself over the edge.

Yorl's home stood starkly against a sky saturated in blue. It was a castle made of stone, with three towers connected by flying buttresses. Sunlight cut through the arid air and reflected off snow in a way that made the gray shale scintillate with shadow and silver.

Cara slipped behind a boulder to rest.

She had served alongside the Koradictine in Arderveer. That assignment had been two hellish months of taking orders from him, watching the way his tongue ran wetly over his bulbous lips every time they met, suffering through his leering smile whenever she first walked into any session, and seeing his strategies fail to achieve what they might have if the mage had the balls to make any real decisions.

Her skin crawled at the mere thought of his touch.

It was *his* ineptitude that let the Torean god-touched mage slip away. Things would have been different if she were in command that day. As it was, she had re-deployed her Lectodinian mages all on her own. Otherwise, they may actually have lost Takril, the Torean ruler of the city, as well as the god-touched.

Still, she was the one who paid for the loss with a stint in the underplanes.

She would not forget that.

Ever.

Cara patted the weapon beneath her bearskin coat. It was a long dagger, magicked in her own laboratory with a sorcery augmented by black powers from those same underplanes she was now so familiar with. It was attuned to Yorl's body. That magic had cost her dearly—she would be paying the demon for months. But it had been worth it. The blade squirmed and made her stomach turn with its corruption. Maybe, she thought, she had done *too* good of a job on it.

Dismissing the thought, she peered around the boulder.

She reached for her link and gathered magical energy about her. As the magestuff flowed, Yorl's castle lit up with wards. Cara pressed her mind to leverage proper points, and she molded sorcery around the foundation of his security spell. With a coordinated pull, she removed their linkages and the Koradictine's magic fell apart.

The hardest part was over.

She straightened and walked to the castle.

The door opened easily. It was warm inside so she removed her bearskin overcoat, leaving the weapon free and available for her left-handed pull. The steel seemed to throb at her side.

Yorl Maggore was immersed in watching a pair of rodents mate when she found him.

His first expression was surprise.

Then, when recognition hit, his smile became its familiar leer.

Her magic flared, showing him an image of her dancing before him, wearing filmy clothes of Koradictine red.

Cara handed him her sword then, and stepped back to watch.

The illusion still smiled, and still danced as it ran fingers through his greasy hair. It kissed him as he gripped the weapon closer with one hand and ran his other hand over her thigh. One of her illusion's ghostly hands drew a line from his sternum, along his neck, and up his jaw bone to his chin. Then slowly, excruciatingly slowly, it lifted his chin skyward to expose the pasty white jugular.

The blade flared purple as he raised it upon himself.

The coppery smell of fresh blood filled the room.

The expression on Yorl's face when Cara left was pure horror.

It made her very happy.

THIRTY

Zutrian Esta stood before a map of the plane he had spread out over the longest wall of his meeting hall, listening carefully as the commanders' reports came in.

The plan was working even better than he hoped.

He had been right to hold his mages back, to regroup and train, and to strike with guerilla forces in the dead of winter when surprise was on his side. A blue flag jutted from the map in each place where a Lectodinian had bested a Koradictine. The map was almost completely filled with them. Over the past week, the raids had systematically removed over two-thirds of the Koradictine order from this side of Adruin.

His revenge was nearly complete.

He grimaced at the red flags pinned to de'Mayer Island. Only Ettril and his small collection of mages remained, so it was upsetting that he could not get a report on Ettril's whereabouts.

But, regardless of whether Ettril Dor-Entfar lived or did not, the Koradictine order would never again be a power on this plane.

So, yes, it was a very good day.

But still, he wondered.

Where could the Koradictine High Superior have gone?

THIRTY-ONE

Hirl-enat spoke to Neuma with an icy edge to his voice. "Who do you think you are? Ettril is gone, and Quin Sar is dead. That leaves me in command here."

Neuma kept her cool and paused for effect, noting Fil's watchful eye. Fil, sitting, as always, in silent examination, was a loyal mage. Fil would ensure everything that happened in this tent would get out to what remained of the order. She hadn't expected Hirl-enat to be this ambitious, but if she played this right, it could work out even better. Garrick would still take care of the Lord Superior, Hirl-enat would be gone, and the order would be hers.

Garrick's absence from Dorfort changed the time scale, so she could be patient with Hirl-enat's petty ego while he painted himself into a corner.

"Who do I think I am?" she said. "I think I'm the one with the plan. But if you have better thoughts for dealing with the Toreans *and* the Lectodinians, then I suggest you put them forward now."

The older mage pursed his lips, his bushy beard bristling around his mouth. She took great delight in his pained expression. The elder wizard was one-upped but didn't want to show it.

The three of them were alone. High Superior Dor-Entfar had disappeared. Worse, while searching for Ettril, they heard reports of mages who suffered scuffles with the Lectodinian sect. She worried about that the most. It meant the Lectodinians—who had emerged from the battle at God's Tower essentially unscathed—had likely decided that the Koradictine order was at its most defenseless now and that Zutrian Esta, High Superior of the Lectodinians, had begun to press his advantage.

If true, it was imperative they get back to Badwall and hold onto the Canyons and their surrounding regions. Otherwise the Koradictine order as they knew it could be swept away.

Neuma's plan was the best they could manage while they were out here in the middle of nowhere. In a nutshell, she suggested they split—one mage casting magic to transport immediately to Badwall and calm disquiet there, the other two taking the several-day journey to the Vapor Peaks to request direct counsel with the Lectodinian leadership.

It was a plan that put Hirl-enat in a difficult situation.

With Ettril gone, Hirl-enat was the ranking Koradictine. As such it was almost mandatory that he perform the role that met with the Lectodinians. Yet, the mage who went home to Badwall would be seen as a leader there, too. Hirl-enat would not want Neuma to have that boon, but they both knew Fil was not strong enough to cast the magic required to perform the transport.

So the gambit was forced upon Hirl-enat. Go to Vapor Peaks and let Neuma run the order in their homeland, or go to Badwall and let Neuma communicate with, and possibly conspire with, their most bitter of rivals.

She wondered which poison he would choose.

"The plan is good as far as it goes," Hirl-enat finally said. "I suggest you return to Badwall while Fil and I work with the Lectodinians. But we will reconsider our path through the Mist Mountains. The directions you selected are inappropriate."

Neuma smiled, knowing Hirl-enat had picked on this portion of the plan merely because it was something he could change. His tinkering would amount to a few ineffectual adjustments based on topography that was probably out of date anyway.

"I see what you mean," she said, gazing at the map.

They worked together for another half hour, refining the plan, then went to their bedrolls. It was time to sleep. They needed to be prepared.

And Neuma *was* tired. The battle with the Toreans had worn her down. But as they walked away, Neuma was uncertain if she would get much sleep at all. The essence of the plan was still *her* work. Fil would ensure the order heard the truth of that.

Whatever happened, tomorrow would be a good day, she thought as she pulled her roll over her shoulder.

Yes.

A very good day.

NESTAFAR

THIRTY-TWO

The robe was gone. Garrick felt that truth before he was fully awake.

He was back in his bed chamber. Back in Dorfort's government center. He smelled the aroma of Blue Lake and heard the sounds of a city working its day. He rose to one elbow and glanced around the room. He was lying on the mattress, his chest bare, his pants Torean black.

The robe was most definitely gone.

He stood and went to the window.

It was early morning. The lake was a calm before the storm, Garrick thought. People milled about the city, each with their simple concerns following them about. Garrick could not help but grimace at his strange mix of emotions. The human experience was so isolated. He missed the sense of connection he had in Existence. Yet, he still felt embarrassed of his attempts to trivialize what these people were feeling as they went about their lives.

He thought of Alistair and wondered what his past superior would think of him now. The question left him feeling bittersweet.

He was surprised to think of himself in this fashion.

He was a man now. A grown man. A full mage, and more.

Garrick felt the full weight of what that meant. He sighed then, realizing he was hungry.

He had to get the Freeborn together. He had to stretch them.

Perhaps, he thought, he had to bring all of the plane's mages under one hand. He had seen what could one day be coming. The mages of Adruin needed to be a single entity, working together if the plane was to survive.

Yes, he had much work to do.

Garrick turned from the window and strode to his closet to pick out a shirt.

"Will!" he called. "Come help me prepare for the day."

THIRTY-THREE

Garrick burst into Ellesadil's chamber. A guard moved to stop him, but Garrick brushed past. He was angry, and the shove was harder than it should have been, but he didn't pause to check on the guard or to apologize for his handling.

"Where is the boy?" Garrick said.

"Garrick?" The lord looked up from his paperwork with an expression of shock that swiftly settled into a relieved smile. He looked old and tired. It was early morning. A bowl of cold cereal and a half cup of the ginger tea he was so famously enamored with sat on one side of his desk. "I'm glad to see you," he said, standing and leaning with both hands on his desk. "Where have you been?"

"Am I to understand the boy is taken by the Koradictines?" Garrick growled, barely able to control himself.

"Yes. You understand correctly," Ellesadil replied.

Garrick turned away, his mind on fire. He could not control himself, though. He turned back to Lord Ellesadil, and in three steps had him by the throat.

He lifted the lord from his chair and pinned him against the wall. Ellesadil's fear tasted cold and bitter against Garrick's hunger.

The lord struggled to breathe, but Garrick didn't care. The boy was gone and it had happened on Ellesadil's watch. Ellesadil put his hands around Garrick's forearm. His face turned pink.

"How did you let this happen?" he said.

"I—" the lord couldn't choke out the rest.

"He was just a boy," Garrick roared, pressing Ellesadil harder against the wall as heat rose within him. "How could you let this happen?"

Ellesadil's face grew even more crimson. The lord's leg kicked meekly before Garrick's rage finally collected itself and he dropped Ellesadil harshly to the floor.

Garrick stood there, panting, towering over the lord with feet spread apart, his arms extended, fingers flexing. The guard came meekly in through the doorway.

"Leave us," Garrick said. "You have my word that Lord Ellesadil will not be harmed."

The guard hesitated, but Ellesadil sat up straighter against the wall, breathed deeply, and waved him away.

"Where did they go?" Garrick said.

"We don't know," Ellesadil replied, holding his hand to his throat and beginning to get his wits about him again. "Darien and Reynard have been patrolling since the boy was kidnapped."

"How long have they been out?"

"Days. Where have you been?"

Garrick closed his eyes, ignoring the lord's question.

His time in Existence had changed him. He felt it the moment he woke up in his chamber. His magic was bigger, more encompassing. He focused on his life force and felt the depths of the world around him with a connection he had never understood before. He smelled the aroma of bread from across town. He sensed a merchant's concern for his daughter who had woken to a fever this morning. He felt how these two things depended on each other, how the fact of one was tied to the fact of the other in the invisible way all actions in all communities of people were tied. But, in the same manner, he felt weary in ways he hadn't before. He was tired of the struggle, deadened to problems that seemed to never end and seemed, perhaps, to never have an end.

"The kidnapping is a message," he said.

"A message?"

Ellesadil stood up.

"They want their revenge on me. This kidnapping says the Koradictines know of my tie to Will."

Ellesadil contemplated Garrick's thought as he edged back to his desk and sipped tea. His unease with Garrick's presence was a thing in itself. "That would explain much."

"The boy is a target because of me. I do not wish to imagine what they might be doing to him now."

"If you are correct, they will hold the boy safe to entice you to come to them."

"Perhaps," Garrick said.

But he had learned much the past year. He had seen the orders close-up and had felt the disruptions that occurred when their power went astray. Garrick felt that same thing in his bones how—he had been corrupted by that power himself, after all. He had returned to Adruin to fulfill his commitment to wrest control of the Freeborn from the clutches of his best friend.

Perhaps the change in him was brought on by exposure to the raw life force of Existence, or perhaps Braxidane—who was now his Mage Superior—had triggered his next progression. Whatever the cause, he *was* different now.

He felt things more deeply.

He understood the orders more fully.

And now he used these two things, spreading himself over the plane, searching for the magic of Ettril Dor-Entfar, Lord Superior of the Koradictine order, and searching for Will.

He felt three guards as they walked their beat. One still smarted from having lost five crowns at a gaming table last evening. Another entertained his friends with stories of a woman. The third was dying of a blackness growing inside his liver, though Garrick was certain he didn't know it, yet.

A young woman bent to a mopping job.

A fisherman cursed nets he had fouled the previous day.

Garrick clenched his hands. His skin crawled, and his stomach swam in a turgid sea. He felt them all, men and women walking in the rutted streets. He sensed Torean magic practiced in the manor yard by an apprentice who was fumbling with a lesser spell, and he felt an adept named Creseda casting layered magic over a wooden wheel—simple work, being done for a paying customer.

Then he felt what he sought.

A mass of Koradictine magic so thick it nearly clogged his throat.

Ettril Dor-Entfar. It had to be the Koradictine leader.

He sensed more in the area. Darien's trail, the residue of battle lust, and the faint casting of Torean magic that went cold. The Koradictine's magic, too, seemed to snap off as if the caster had just disappeared.

The Koradictine had clearly left the plane.

Garrick went to the window again in a distracted fog. His senses, still stretching across the land, felt heavy and damp.

"Are you going to answer me?" Ellesadil said.

"They'll not find Ettril," Garrick replied.

His mind snapped back into focus.

Ellesadil was fully recovered now. He stood behind his desk and rearranged his disheveled clothing.

"I'm sorry, Lord. I shouldn't have treated you harshly," Garrick said, rubbing his temple. "What was that you said?"

"I asked where you have been."

"I was pulled away by my superior," Garrick said.

It was not a lie. Braxidane had sent him to Rastella to break Hezarin's hold on that plane and to save Braxidane's unborn champion. His work had been successful, and as a reward (or was it a lesson?) he had spent untold hours (or was it days?) immersed in the flowing networks of Existence, the connective tissue between the planes that were home to planewalkers like Braxidane and Hezarin.

Will's disappearance wasn't Ellesadil's fault at all, Garrick saw that clearly. It wasn't Darien's fault, either. Or Reynard's, or anyone else's.

It was his fault. All of it. His fault.

Ettril was able to kidnap Will because Garrick, wasn't here to protect him. And, the abrupt ending to Ettril's path told him that the task of bringing Will back was all his, too. Neither Darien nor Reynard nor any other mage or warrior could follow the Koradictine through the planes.

"Much has happened while you were gone," Ellesadil said.

"We can discuss those things when I return," Garrick replied, striding to the doorway. "But now I need to go find the boy."

"Your order is falling apart, Garrick," the lord said. "You should stay here and mend it."

Garrick gazed at Ellesadil, suddenly feeling more at ease than he could ever remember feeling. He could play the planewalker's game as well as Braxidane could. Garrick had promised to take the Freeborn House from Darien, but there had been no timeline attached to that commitment.

"The world has existed without a Torean order for a long time," he said. "I think it will manage to get by without one for a few days more."

Then Garrick left, his boots echoing in the hallway.

THIRTY-FOUR

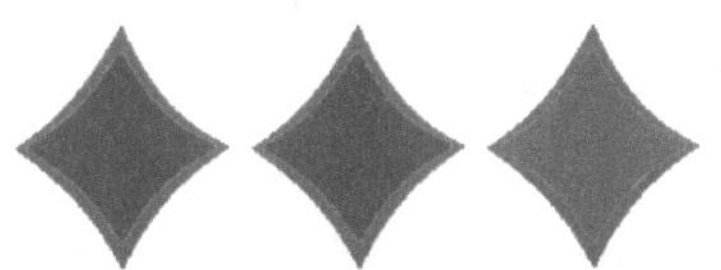

Bare sycamore and birch trees stood as sentries over ground that had been trod upon recently. The wind had calmed to leave the area silent.

Garrick was no ranger, but it took no great expertise to make out the marks of hooves and boot heels that marked the Koradictine campfire. The rut of wagon wheels and prints made by the steady gait of horses were clean signs leading northwest toward the Koradictine stronghold.

But that was not the trail that interested him.

The trail he searched for was the bloody taint of sorcery that he felt decaying up ahead of him, laying dead like residue washed up on a beach. And, along with that blood taint, the path he sought also felt the power that gave Existence its very presence, a sensation that hummed with the essence of life force that, having now experienced it, he would never be able to miss again.

The link told Garrick he was right, that Ettril had left the plane. Could he follow it?

The idea excited him. He felt the link as if it were a physical thing, a vine or a tendril left behind that Garrick could latch onto with his own life force. Its whisper seduced him.

If, as Braxidane said, a planewalker who steps into the realm of a plane opens that door for other planewalkers, would the same policy exist in the opposite direction? Could Ettril's passage leave him room to follow?

Garrick called on his link and drew sorcerous power from Talin's reservoir of magic, channeling it through proper leverage points and letting it pool in his hands until his fingertips glowed golden hot. He molded life force to recreate the sensation of wearing the robe he had found on Rastella. A shell of energy wrapped about him and, when the moment felt complete, Garrick attached his spell to Ettril Dor-Entfar's trail.

Then he pulled.

A BITING wind whined with the dry rasp of dead leaves spinning through the air. The honey-laced aroma of Braxidane's magic grew around Garrick, as intoxicating and sweet as candy. Ettril's trail grew thick. Its essence whipped suddenly around his wrist, attaching to him like a sea serpent's tentacle. It ripped him from the plane, drawing him up and off the land, into a haze that grew dense and damp around him.

This time he was ready, though.

As he stepped into the raging flow of Existence, he drew the hardened mantle of his life force around him. The flow rushed past with a siren's call of raw pleasure.

Something hit his shoulder, and the link snapped with a loud crack. Garrick screamed as he crashed against a hard surface. Fire burst around him. His hands burned as the link tore into the soft meat of his hands. He fell, then, slipping into a vortex of color, spinning out of control.

UNTIL HE FOUND himself kneeling on solid ground.

He was in open plains land under a sky that crackled with electric bolts. Rock and mud surrounded him. Scattered patches of fire crackled from the debris of his passage. He stood, his hunger suddenly strong and vicious inside him. Blood seeped from scrapes and cuts over most of his body. The muscles of his arms, shoulders, and legs burned, and his sweat-damped hair clung to his skull and his neck. A trail of that same perspiration trickled down his back.

Where was he?

Where was Ettril? He couldn't sense the Koradictine.

A movement came at his periphery.

There were things here, beings, creatures, crosses between man and cricket—demons, perhaps—cold and dark and blue, angular, with jutting ridges above gleaming orange eyes and with backs that were hunched up and cowled. They peered at him with hungry curiosity, shielding themselves from the flames that still sputtered around him.

Garrick set spell gates and tried to latch onto the flow of magestuff again. He cast fire at them, but it sputtered randomly.

One demon-thing went rigid, its head thrown back, its mouth opened in a toothless scream. Another creature reached toward Garrick, scoring his arm with a frigid touch that brought Garrick's energy sluicing forward to heal.

Another creature closed in.

He cast his sputtering fire once again, and the thing burned readily. He felt his hunger rise, too, and this time he welcomed it, letting it loose as far as he could. Others pressed in, sucking greedily at the life force that seemed to seep from him at an ever greater pace. And as they absorbed that energy they died. He cast fire and electric flares of power, but still the creatures flowed toward him, dancing and jumping like frenzied insects across the vastness of the horizon.

There were so many.

So many.

He felt his hunger rising from the depths of his life force, but it was sluggish and slow. If he didn't do something soon, Garrick would not be long for this plane.

He fanned energy before him, turning it from simple bolts to beams of lightning, fire, and smoke that flashed with blue and silver streaks. He smelled the creatures' charred exoskeletons and heard their dying screams. Still, they came, mindlessly throwing themselves into the beams, their empty carcasses building into a dark ridge that encircled him. Each wave pressed closer, though. The bodies of their brothers and sisters shielded them as they pressed in.

Garrick whirled against the ever-closing arc, grabbing fistfuls of pure magestuff and throwing it into the fray. He ignored the chattering cries of the creatures that had grown into a wall of macabre laughter. In the back of his mind, he sensed the trail of Koradictine magic leading away.

That was it.

Ettril had known Garrick would follow. He had led him here as a trap, hoping that the creatures would drain his power.

A coldness stole more life from him.

He didn't have time to think further.

Garrick gave the pressing wave of cricket demons a strong spray of flames. The demon creatures shied back. Gleaming eyes grew larger, their stink more fetid.

He used the break to concentrate on the Koradictine's trail.

As the wall of creatures came forward again, Garrick's sorcery latched onto Ettril's pathway.

A demon leaped at him.

Garrick swung his fist and the thing fell into the path of three others that had also been flying toward him. He tugged on the link and lifted himself from the throng. He poured what magestuff he could into the spell, and it raised him farther up. Once certain he was free, Garrick gave a final look downward. A vast ocean of the creatures stared upward, their enormous mouths gaping open like an endless field filled with holes of hungry blackness.

THIRTY-FIVE

Garrick found himself in a chamber that was roughly square in shape. It was a library of some kind. He was confused, but alert. Finding nothing of immediate danger here, he checked his link to the plane of magic. Feeling it still there, he calmed himself.

The muscles across his back ached, and he felt empty inside. His palms were flayed. His life force was drained so deeply that it wasn't healing him now.

Garrick scanned the room.

Each corner was beveled to make it eight-sided, and each of the longer walls was lined with wooden shelves stained to a golden-brown glow. They were filled with tomes and manu-scripts. A full-height closet stood in one corner. A maroon rug covered the floor, its weave reminding him of those that came from Farvane. The rug's padding was thick. It drank up sound so fully that his movements felt slow. The books were of varied sizes and colors, some bound in leather, others simple loose-leaf collections.

The only opening was a doorway across the room.

The trail to Ettril Dor-Entfar, and, therefore to Will, led through that door.

Something didn't seem right, though. His skin crawled with an eerie sense of recognition. He felt like he had been here before.

He stepped across the rug and into the doorway.

The knob turned smoothly.

He pushed the door open to find another room, this one larger, perhaps a sitting room.

The clipped sound of a spoon on porcelain echoed from inside.

Then again.

The floor here was polished hardwood, and his footsteps rang out as he stepped inside. Raw sunlight spilled through windows that were taller than wide. The sun was high, its rays, loaded with dust motes that floated in ghostly waves, were dagger strikes against the linen tablecloth. A high-backed chair sat at the nearest end of a long table, facing away from him. More chairs sat empty along its length. The chair at the table's foot was empty, also. A stick of incense smoldered from an otherwise empty crystal vase at the table's center.

The place smelled of ginger, with a touch of mint—the flavor of Sunathri's magic, he remembered.

Garrick knit his brows.

"Will?" he said, his voice echoing.

The porcelain clatter came again.

From the other side of the chair, Garrick caught the wisp of gray hair. The memory of Ettril's face in Sunathri's communications spell came to him.

"Where is the boy, Ettril?" Garrick said.

His only answer was another thick clink.

Garrick stepped forward.

"You can't run forever," he said.

As the angle changed, though, Garrick saw more of the person sitting in the chair. The man's hair was pure white, almost silver in the natural light of the sun. His skin looked thin and grainy, as if it was cast of dried sugar and as if a good rain might melt it away. The man's hand shook as he moved the spoon to his lips. The meal was a vegetable broth of some kind.

Garrick's heart pounded.

It was another trap. It had to be. But, what harm could this man do him?

"Who are you?" he asked as he stood taller.

The man gave no answer.

"I asked you a question."

His voice died in the open room. Smoke from the incense continued to coil upward.

The man reached for his napkin, and dabbed his lips. A goblet of wine, red, sat on the table next to a saucer covered with bread-crumbs. A short knife smeared with butter also rested upon it.

The man turned his gaze to Garrick with a slowness that was painful. In the instant their gazes locked, Garrick realized who this man was. He recognized the black garments. He saw the curve of his nose and the way his lips turned downward at the corners of his mouth. In that instant Garrick realized he was seeing himself aged beyond recognition, sitting quietly in an empty room with nothing but a smoldering stick of incense to remind himself of who he had once been.

He was alone.

He had always been alone in so many ways.

A groan escaped his lips unbidden.

He wanted to turn his gaze away, but he couldn't. He had to see this no matter how bad it might be. He had always been afraid to open himself up to the world, afraid to be exposed. It was a well-earned paranoia, of course. Life is not arranged to help the defenseless. But there had been times, hadn't there? Moments as a boy growing up in Alistair's manor, times with the other apprentices. Times together with Darien and with Sunathri, yes, times with Sunathri where he could have let his guard down and become the person he truly was.

But he had not been able to do it.

Smoke from the incense grew into a shell around him, and his self-loathing gave that shell a substance that doubled back to drive a stake through his heart.

His isolation was his own fault.

Braxidane's dark hunger rose to fill him. *You are not alone*, it said. *I am here.*

"That's not what I want!" Garrick yelled aloud.

He stepped toward the fragile shell of his older self. The man's hand came toward him, decrepit and brittle, palm upward, forefinger extended, shriveled to nothing but bone draped in sagging skin.

"Don't leave me," his elder self said, his voice wavering and reedy.

Visceral panic mixed with fear. Garrick swept his hand blindly along the table.

The wine glass spilt.

Broth splattered onto the elder's lap.

It was like shedding weight, like waking from a long sleep, like breathing again after being underwater for his entire life. The smoke shimmered around him.

The aged hand crooked its index finger again, twisting its call to the hunger inside him, drawing it closer. Garrick felt the thing's appetite, it's longing for something else to take, something else to feed into its loneliness if only for as long as it took to digest it.

He grabbed the knife from the table and swung it against the old man's arm. The hand snapped off and twirled through the air.

An expression of shocked betrayal came over the elder's face. His lips drew into jagged wrinkles that ran from his cheekbones to his chin. The hunger they shared sucked life force into it. The old Garrick reached with his other hand, fingers cupped in a needful curl.

Garrick slashed again, sending this hand tumbling also.

He hacked at his old self then, pouring life force into his short blade. The edge caught sharp sunlight and glinted with a natural flare. Its brilliant reflections danced across the ceiling and along the walls as Garrick stabbed and slashed, again and again until what used to be his older self was reduced to a pile of dust that spread across the floor like sand.

His blood pounded in his chest.

Sweat beaded at his brow.

Garrick stood still, his body limp, his muscles weak.

His hunger rolled inside him in huge, welling waves that crashed against the inside of his head.

The incense no longer smoked.

The table sat at an odd angle, its broken chairs scattered about.

This entire place was an elaborate hoax Ettril had left in hopes that Garrick would fall prey to his own self-loathing. He shook his head to clear the idea, but Ettril's magic was so strong that even the act of understanding what was happening did not enable Garrick to rid himself of the ominous weight of the room.

Garrick turned to the open door.

"Will," he said, focusing to find the dim thread he knew would lead wherever Ettril was taking him. It was a low, pulsing line of magic he found. Slight, but clear.

"Hold on, Will," he said. "I'm coming."

THIRTY-SIX

Ettril sat on a high-backed chair at the top of a marble tower in the grandest castle across the land, waiting. His mind registered every rippling sensation within the flow of the plane.

Nestafar was perfect.

It was a small place of little note, but one with enough energy to serve his purposes. He would use it to destroy the Torean god-touched. In this way, he would raise Nestafar from its obscurity to ensure it a place in the histories of mankind—Nestafar, the plane where the Freeborn heard their death knell. Not a bad footnote, he thought.

Surely more than the plane had deserved *before* he arrived.

Ettril looked at the boy, Will, who lay sprawled on a pallet across the room. He had made the mistake of letting Will regain consciousness once and paid for that error with a barrage of questions that might never have stopped if he hadn't beaten the boy to silence. Now Will was trussed up. His head lolled to one side, and his mouth was gagged.

An image of Hirl-enat came to him, coated with a sensation of urgency.

He brushed it away.

He could get used to being god-touched. His was the only true magic on this plane, and he was the only creature with a link to Talin, the only one with the Touch of Existence.

Well, the only human, he thought with a smile.

Hirl-enat's image persisted, though, pulling at him with a dogged determination that said the mage wasn't going away. Ettril spoke a few words of magic and made a connection.

"I hope for your sake this is important," he said.

"Are you all right, Lord? We've been unable to raise you."

Ettril smiled. "I am more than all right. Tell me what this is about."

Hirl-enat paused for only the slightest of moments.

"Lectodinian raiders are destroying our order, sir."

"Lectodinians?" Ettril turned his full attention to his Koradictine subordinate. "Tell me more."

"We've been polling the order as you asked, and one after the other has been unable to answer. Those who can, however, report of murdered mages left amid traces of Lectodinian magic."

Ettril cursed. He cast a burst of magic that twisted across his palms in a caustic blue-brown cloud.

"Zutrian thinks he's found us weakened," he said.

"He may be right, Superior. I've been able to rouse only two mages. We need you back here now."

"No!" Ettril's anger flared again.

Hezarin would be furious if he left this task undone, and after all this time he would not deny himself the sweet anticipation he felt toward seeing Garrick squirm.

Beyond that, his god-touch had let him see things in a different light. He had been so wrong about so many things throughout his life. He once thought events on Adruin mattered, that controlling people and obtaining power there was important. But his travels through All of Existence and the taste of this new power were enough to change all that.

He drew energy from his link, reveling in the purity of its strength. Let Zutrian have his day in the sun, he thought.

Garrick was on his way. It would not be long now.

"This is my moment of revenge. I'll not have it wasted by a petty Lectodinian who thinks he understands power."

"But if you don't come now, the Koradictines—"

"I said no." Ettril's voice was sharp as a battle axe. "Take care of this yourself. I will return when I can, and I'll expect the order to be in proper condition."

He shut down the communication link and gathered himself.

Ettril motioned toward the boy and felt life force waft with an aroma as attractive as fresh-baked pie.

The boy moaned.

He turned his attention back to his spell work, tending the trail he had left to float free. It felt odd to be the bait of his own trap, odd, but wonderful at the same time. It made him feel important. It made him feel like he was in control—which, of course, he was.

Energy crackled around him—azure and cobalt, lavender, golden chartreuse, browns of soil, and greens of the forests.

Yes, Ettril thought.

He was after far larger prey.

Adruin could wait.

THIRTY-SEVEN

The Koradictine's link grew stronger and easier to follow as it led Garrick back through Existence. He gathered up life force as it flowed over him. Its vitality filled him. It brought him renewed vigor.

"Don't you have an order to run?"

Garrick recognized the tone of superiority in Braxidane's voice.

"Can't you see I'm busy?" he replied.

"I can see you're wasting your time on things that are unimportant."

"Will is not unimportant."

"I think you need to prioritize better."

"I know what I'm doing."

"Then perhaps you can explain why the leader of an order of mages is letting that same order crumble rather than face his responsibility."

"You wouldn't understand."

"Wouldn't I?"

"Compassion is not an emotion you're familiar with."

"I am apparently as familiar with compassion as you are with accountability."

"I'll do things on my time, Braxidane. Now get out of my way. I have better things to do than argue with you. You're causing me to lose touch with the Koradictine."

Garrick set his gates and drew upon the plane of magic.

The thread grew more substantial, and he pulled on it to find himself rushing through the gray matter of Existence once again.

A dark gate loomed ahead.

He slipped into it, and a blast furnace of flaming energy rose around him—Ettril's ward. He dug into the flow to bring up a shield of free energy. The gate was strong. It tasted bold and sharp, like dark tea left burning too long.

This would be it.

Ettril had run long enough, and the strength of this ward told Garrick this was where Ettril Dor-Entfar would make his stand.

"How do you think he's doing it?" Braxidane asked.

Garrick grimaced, sensing his superior's trail beside him. "I thought I left you behind."

Braxidane hung in the flow like a bulbous jellyfish, saying nothing, biding his time.

"Doing what?" Garrick asked as he probed the ward.

"How do you think the Koradictine is traveling the planes so easily?"

Garrick thought about that. He couldn't have survived Existence his first time without the protection of Karasacti's robe. How was Ettril Dor-Entfar doing it?

"You don't know, do you?" Braxidane's voice picked at him like he was a piece of meat. "Typical. You went charging off to save the world without a thought about what you were up against."

"I did the best I knew how."

"That excuse doesn't work anymore, Garrick. You should know that by now. You need to act as if you understand things are bigger than Adruin."

"He's getting help," Garrick said, beginning to realize what Braxidane was telling him.

"Yes. My sister is supporting him."

"So is he god-touched now?"

"She can't have another god-touched on Adruin," Braxidane said. "But, yes, so long as he isn't on that plane—or on any other plane that has an existing mage she has ... touched—Ettril Dor-Entfar is now hers."

A sense of fatigue washed over Garrick.

"This is all Hezarin's doing, then? The whole Koradictine uprising? Rastella, stealing Will? It's all on her shoulders."

"You're growing brighter with every passing moment," Braxidane said. "I am so proud."

"So once again we're merely planewalkers' proxies."

"Humans have never needed planewalkers to find cause to combat each other."

"Ettril couldn't have gotten off Adruin without her."

"There are many ways to cross planes."

"That's what I like about you, Braxidane. You're always so firm in your answers."

"It's an unsteady universe, Garrick. You'll just have to deal with it."

Garrick chewed on that as the current pulled on them. Streaks of color passed, scarlet, and yellow, and the blue of a jay's wing. He was no longer the boy who had been sold to Alistair, no longer the young man who had proposed to his love in the woods.

He laughed at himself.

"This is certain, Braxidane: I *am* going to get Will back. You can't dissuade me of that."

"You've got one simple task, Garrick. One. Lead the Freeborn. It's a task of great value, yet you will risk yourself and everything you mean to Adruin merely to save a boy?"

"I have to, or I cannot lead the Freeborn."

"I cannot help you from this point."

"Can't or won't?"

"I've already given Hezarin the upper hand by intervening once when you would surely have died. I can't afford to do it again."

"So it's *won't*."

"I don't understand you, Garrick."

"That's not my concern."

Braxidane turned slate gray, and dipped a row of gaseous cilia to flow freely in the currents.

Then Garrick was alone.

He smiled to himself. It felt good.

Then he turned back to the gate.

He had been letting the Koradictine dictate their path, and in doing so had been letting him set his traps. The first had drained his life force, the second had dealt a blow to his psyche. Both had caught him by surprise. That couldn't happen again.

He used these last few moments to absorb what strength he could. Then he set his gates and gathered life force within him. The two magics folded in upon each other. He trembled with their forces as he wrapped them around himself to create a protective covering that shone brightly throughout All of Existence.

Then Garrick stepped through the portal.

THIRTY-EIGHT

Garrick landed in a blazing ball of fire.

This place had once been a city, but was now charred and blackened. Tall buildings of architecture that spoke of an artistic people were fallen in shambles, bricks crumbled, stones cracked and splintered to expose their coarse innards.

Bodies littered the ground.

Men and women. Children. Dogs, horses, mules, and cattle. They all lay shriveled and decaying, leaving the city to smell of burnt flesh.

His stomach churned with bile. Garrick had seen this before.

He felt a presence behind him at the same time as he heard the moan, a low, familiar cry that grew to a high-pitched wail.

Garrick turned.

"Alistair," he said.

His old mage superior stood on a platform of charred stone with an ugly blue energy swirling about him like a bruised cloud. His staff was in one hand, his arms outstretched. Ettril had loosed Alistair on the people here, letting him feed upon the whole of this world's citizens—a foul trick, given Alistair's inability to draw real sustenance.

Garrick pushed his senses outward, hoping to see where the

Koradictine superior had fled, following the single thread of power that led toward Ettril and toward Will.

The path went directly through Alistair.

He wondered how Ettril had found his old superior, but in the end realized that it didn't matter at all. Perhaps it was Hezarin's doing. Perhaps not. What mattered was that Garrick had created this thing that was now Alistair, and that Alistair had done this wicked deed. And what mattered was that Garrick had to find a way past Alistair if he was going to get to Will.

"I've made a mess of you," Garrick said. "Of that, I'm sorry."

Alistair's voice screeched in the wind. He waved a staff that glowed ugly green. An aching need grew from nowhere to draw on Garrick from every direction.

A woman's arm moved, flaking with skin of ashes and oozing with dark fluid. A man stood up, his face peeling from his skull. They rose like that, more and more of them, tens of the dead at a time, then hundreds, bones clattering, teeth against teeth, wailing with dry, creaking screeches.

Alistair waved his staff again and their eye sockets filled with need.

These people were damned, their life forces destroyed in some obscene fashion. Their cold desire snaked between them as if they were a single thing.

Garrick set gates and drew on his link to Talin. He leaped to the tallest pedestal of stone, and fire flared from his fist. Lightning flashed from Alistair's staff. The explosion of their meeting rocked the ground. A bony hand wrapped itself around Garrick's ankle with a touch that burned so cold he thought the flesh had been flayed from the bone.

Garrick turned his fire on it.

He couldn't hold back and expect to survive, so he channeled life force to form a long-bladed sword of pure energy built of Existence itself, and he rained it down on anything close to him. Everything it touched burned, and everywhere it went Alistair's zombies gave their final screams.

His foot throbbed as he fought.

He had expected his life force to heal whatever wounds he suffered, but it did no good against the zombie's touch. Hobbling and gritting his teeth, he faced Alistair with even deeper respect.

Alistair prepared another spell.

Garrick leaped into the mass of blackened bodies, cutting a swath through them with wild swings of his sword. He paid a dear price, though. Each strike drew his energy down. He skewered a woman, then spun and destroyed a line of charred bodies.

Alistair cast magic after magic.

Garrick's power drained further.

Two snakes, huge and bulbous, raised their hooded heads and spit vile globs of blackness at Garrick. The poison sizzled as it flew through the air. Garrick reached out with raw magic, grabbed zombies, and threw them into the poison's path, ducking under clouds of ash that formed as they were struck.

Garrick slashed his way farther across the field, weaving, spinning, and ducking in a battlefield ballet. Sweat poured from his aching body, and he no longer thought. There was only him, only his enemies, and only the sword that seemed tied to him like a brother.

The snakes closed in, and one whipped its tail at Garrick.

He leapt away and jammed his blade into the beast's mouth.

The other was behind him and took advantage of the moment to close its jaws over Garrick's chest, its ichor-covered fangs sliding past his rib. It raised its head and screamed with anger as it shook him.

Garrick stared into its dead, black eye, and poured life force into the blade as he raked the weapon over the snake's head.

Its body gave a spasm, and he poured more fire into this new wound, rending it deeply, then splitting it in two. The reptile faded and fell dead to the ground, dropping Garrick into a free fall. He twisted, barely able to get his good leg under him before he hit the ground.

More zombies pressed in.

Alistair was nearby now. Close.

Garrick fought with a mindless sense of survival. He forgot about Will or Ettril. He forgot about the Freeborn, forgot about Darien, Reynard, or Sunathri. For that moment there was no future. No past. Only now, and only here, and there were only blackened bodies that stung with deadly cold, and there was only a weapon that pulverized his opponent if he could just get it between them.

Alistair chanted a steady stream of magic. His skin hung from his face in limpid pools of decay. A hole in his jaw showed three blackened teeth, and the pupils of his eyes glowed an unreal green.

Garrick's life force flowed as he fought his way through the mass of Alistair's zombie army.

Then he was on the dais with his past master.

He swung his sword of pure life force to meet Alistair's staff. They crashed in a shower of eternally blue sparks, and the staff splintered like driftwood.

The mass of black creatures paused.

Garrick's arm felt dead.

Alistair's expression became filled with hatred. A grated whisper leaked from his rotted mouth.

Garrick recognized that sound.

Alistair was focusing on magic, verbalizing distantly memorized favorites from the time when he was Garrick's superior, teaching again. Alistair was always teaching.

Garrick transferred his sword to his good hand, searching Alistair's eyes for something that looked familiar but seeing nothing beyond blackness and pain.

Screaming, Garrick buried the blade in Alistair's chest.

He pushed life force into the hilt, using the weapon to inject it into Alistair, flooding him in a single release of raw anger that had built since the day his superior had been taken from him.

The blast was immense.

A ball of white fire tossed Garrick backward.

Maybe he screamed again, but any sound he made was dwarfed by the explosion that filled all space and all time.

Then everything was silent.

He lay on his back, trying without success to rise up. He was spent. Done for.

Finally, sound came to him, a wind moaned its way through buildings that towered above. He had to find his sword. He had to find Alistair. He had to find Will.

Will?

Who was Will?

Finally, he rolled to one side, and his fine hair fell like a cobweb over his face. He tried to blow it away, tried to swipe at it with his hand, but nothing moved like it should.

Then, slowly, everything faded to black.

THIRTY-NINE

A sensation of movement came over Ettril Dor-Entfar.

It was Garrick, he realized, the wrinkle Garrick made in the fabric of this little plane upon his arrival in Nestafar.

He sensed the intensity of the battle between Garrick and Alistair.

He felt the web of the plane split with each spell casting, felt the zombies' hunger—a hunger that was unsurprising in its desperation given that he, Ettril Dor-Entfar, had already absorbed every bit of life force on the plane. The creatures would ache forever, but this was of little consequence to him. He felt Garrick's triumph over the snakes, the Torean god-touched sense of achievement at reaching Alistair. The inclusion of Garrick's previous superior in this game was a masterful stroke that had raised the plan from merely a satisfying work of substance to a rare piece of art.

The final explosion startled him.

He gazed again at the boy, still shackled and unconscious.

All that sacrifice for a single child. It made no sense.

There was nothing special about him. He was small, with freckles over his nose. He wasn't particularly well-kept. He had no foreseeable future. No, Ettril thought, it made no sense at all that Garrick would go to these lengths to save an orphaned boy such as Will.

He felt Garrick's life force fade as the Torean lay on the cold surface of the Nestafarian tundra.

He stood then.

The time had come to play his last gambit. The time had come for him to claim his eternal right.

FORTY

Garrick felt as if he had been whipped a thousand times. He was cold. His vision was a blur. His mind numb.

He thought his foot had been shredded, and he wasn't certain he even had a left hand anymore.

His hunger was like a creature gnawing inside him.

He had fallen. He remembered that.

And Alistair.

He remembered Alistair, remembered the dead look in his superior's eyes just before he broke into a thousand pieces. At least Alistair's pain was over, he thought. At least there was that.

He scanned the battlefield without moving his head.

Debris scattered in the wind. Tatters of cloth and paper blew in eddy currents. The smell of burned and rotted flesh seemed the only presence left on the plane.

Against this backdrop, Ettril Dor-Entfar glided into his view.

At first, the Koradictine was a speck on the horizon, distant and tiny, moving with what appeared to be ant-like speed. But he drew near quickly, and Garrick saw that he traveled on a disk that glimmered with scintillating mage flame, riding him forward like a magic carpet. His crimson robes, with their golden-threaded brocade, were anachronisms amid the blacks and grays of the rest of the plane.

As the mage drew nearer, Garrick saw another disk followed behind. It, too, glowed blue, and it, too, hovered inches from the ground.

Will lay in a pitiful heap upon it.

Will.

The boy rolled to look at Garrick, his eyes wide and his mouth gagged. His thin arms were tied firmly against his sides, his hands bound behind his back.

Garrick's heart plunged. He raised himself to an elbow, wincing with the effort.

Braxidane! Garrick gave a desperate call through his link. *Braxidane!*

There was no response.

He struggled to draw his legs underneath him, pleased to see his foot, though swollen and bloodied, remained intact. The movement came with pain, though, and his limbs were jelly.

Garrick looked once more at Will, and anger fueled his strength.

He stood, his legs trembling.

He held his ribs awkwardly, his hand numb against his belly. His life force sputtered like a candle drowning in its own wax. He set a gate and felt a gentle trickle that dulled his pain but could not remove it.

Ettril towered over him amid the rubble of this devastated city. The intensity of his presence burned against Garrick's hunger like a raging sun. That hunger surged with the Koradictine's nearness. It wanted to drink Ettril in, to reach out and take him as it had once taken a serving lad in a village outside Dorfort, to rip Ettril's life force from his body as he once had done to mages on the fields of God's Tower. But Ettril Dor-Entfar was no simple mage. He was god-touched himself, and he was having none of Garrick's fantasies.

"If you harmed the boy," Garrick said, his tongue clay in his mouth, "I'll kill you."

Ettril gave a deep belly laugh. Energy crackled across the Kora-dictine's entire being.

"I'm so pleased to find you're still alive," Ettril said, his voice echoing inside Garrick's skull.

Ettril seemed larger than life. His staff flowed like liquid in his hand, and he smiled with vile humor as he took in the destruction that lay around him. His silver-gray hair shifted and waved of its own volition. His skin glowed. His eyes were puffy, white, and bloated, their pupils dilated and wild.

"It wasn't Alistair who drained the plane at all, was it?" Garrick said, shivering with the cold wind. The trickle of mage stuff was helping him. At least he could stand on his own. "You're the one who created these creatures."

"Weren't they wonderful?" Ettril said.

"But now you have no one to rule."

"I never intended to rule Nestafar, Garrick."

Garrick was aghast. "You destroyed an entire plane on a lark?"

"I destroyed it because I needed its energy, and because I needed someplace to draw you toward." He glanced around and gave a smile, his lips full and pulsing. "So, in a way, you could say Nestafar's fate was your fault. Isn't that just ... perfect?"

"These people were merely mage fodder to you?"

"It was a selfish plane, anyway," Ettril said, "filled with people interested in wealth and material rather than knowledge. Their greed had already changed the very composition of their plane. So, you see, I didn't really do anything they weren't already doing to themselves."

"You spout Hezarin's credo like an expert," Garrick said.

"Only because she's right. I've done this plane a great service. Now it can rebuild itself."

"You are generous to a fault."

"I'm glad you see it that way. It will make it more pleasant to think of you when I use your life force someplace else."

The blow came almost from nowhere, but Garrick was schooled

enough to react as soon as he smelled the Koradictine odor rising within the fabric of the plane's existence. He pulled as much magic into his mind as he could and threw a shield haphazardly over himself.

Still, the Koradictine's fist of power tossed him to the ground like a rag doll.

Garrick took refuge behind the cornerstone of a broken building. Ettril's god-touch was strong, his magic sizzled with vitality. Garrick would never beat him if this battle came down to sorcerous power. His only chance was to somehow nab Will, and get off the plane.

"Come out from behind that rock," Ettril said. "You know you can't hide from me anymore."

Gripping the boulder, Garrick stood up again, strangely ready to die. It would be worth it if he could save Will, he thought. And it would solve so many problems.

Energy seeped from the Koradictine.

Garrick's hunger was drawn to that energy. It yearned for its sustenance and drew morsels from its fringe.

Will squirmed on the disc, obviously understanding what was happening around him.

"The two of you share a bond," Ettril said with clear distaste. "So, to prove I can be accommodating, I'll take both of you at the same time."

Ettril sang a phrase, and magic swirled in the clouds above him.

Garrick took the moment to grab what little energy he could, and he threw a bolt at the disk where Will lay. The leather around the boy's wrists scorched, and the bindings around his arms burned away.

"Run, Will," Garrick said.

The boy rolled from the disk, wasting no time. He ripped the gag from his mouth as he ran, falling once, then getting up to run again.

"You think I won't be able to find him later?" Ettril said, turning back to cast his spell.

A black cone struck Garrick full in the chest, and every muscle in his body clenched.

An avalanche of cascading pain crushed him.

His heart stopped. Bones ground against bones. His teeth gritted with the bloody taste of calcium and saliva. He fell, gasping for breath and groaning with distended sounds he had never heard from himself before.

The ground was hard against his cheek and temple.

Shards of the city lay around him—broken panes of glass and metal, a blackened piece of cloth, scraps of wood that had once been a chair or a bed or maybe just a table.

After all this, Garrick thought, he was going to die alone on a distant plane. Fitting, he supposed. He crawled toward the Koradictine, his bleeding fingers pulling himself along the ground. It hurt merely to breathe, but he wanted to give Will time to run.

Ettril strode forward until the hem of his robe filled Garrick's vision.

"You are weak," Ettril said.

"Uhhh ..." was all he could manage in response.

Then he saw Will, sneaking up behind the mage, holding a jagged piece of metal in his grimy hand, his eyes hard and cold like no child's should ever be.

No! he thought to Will. *You're supposed to run! You're supposed to get away.*

But the boy did not turn to run. Instead, Will crept farther toward the Koradictine.

So Garrick did the only thing he could. He pressed against the ground, lifting himself to stand before Ettril Dor-Entfar.

"You are pitiful," the Koradictine said.

Will raised his makeshift weapon and aimed for a place between Ettril's shoulder blades.

He was too late, though.

The Koradictine's energy rose. Ettril whirled and faced the boy, his expression an evil contortion of humor and disdain.

"You didn't think I would actually give you my back, did you?" he said, raising his arm to cast his death spell.

Garrick went red with rage.

"Noooooooooooo ..."

He rose up, then. He forgot about Braxidane, or about sorcery, or about Talin, the plane of magic. He ignored dead muscles and biting hunger. He rose up, arms and legs screaming with pain—rose up, wailing like the demons wailed as he entered their plane of blue. He rose up, lifting a rock the size of Ettril's head, a remnant of a wall, or perhaps a bank, a shop, a brothel, a tavern, or a bench that once served as a place to rest, or, perhaps maybe just a cornerstone to what had served as the home of a simple family. He rose with a rock from Nestafar that became an extension of his arm. And he hefted it, swinging it as if there was nothing left in the world but that chunk of granite. And he released it, his arm swinging forward, his muscles stretching with satisfying ache.

The rock flew through the air with natural grace.

It crashed into Ettril's skull as the Koradictine's spell hit its leverage point. Bone gave with a sickening crunch. The odor of Koradictine sorcery rose and then fell.

As that stone fell, a pair of voices screamed, one the voice of age, the other of youth. And as it fell, Ettril Dor-Entfar's magic went astray and exploded against a stone wall in the distance.

Garrick tumbled to the ground.

Then there was silence.

FORTY-ONE

Garrick opened his eyes to see white clouds sliding across the sky like smoke. For the first time in forever, it felt like he was warm.

Strange, he thought. So strange.

Something speared his kidney, though, and his foot felt like it was being crushed under a mountain. He clenched his fist and gasped with pain that pierced his entire being. If he didn't know better, he would have thought he had been taken apart piece by piece.

A warm sensation picked at his mind.

Then he saw Will.

The boy lay motionless against a stone wall. Ettril Dor-Entfar was facedown a distance away, a trail of blackening blood running from his head to form a clotted pool in a bowl-like depression at his side.

Garrick groaned.

His hunger stirred. It strained against him, drawing him toward Will's life force. It urged Garrick to stand, to walk, to crawl, to do whatever it took to absorb this fresh power. He bottled that hunger, though. He was stronger than it now. It laughed at him from its depths, though. It would have its way sometime, he knew. But that sometime would not be today.

He crawled to the boy's side.

Will's breathing rattled in his chest. His skin was clammy, but he was alive.

"Braxidane!" Garrick yelled aloud. "Braxidane!"

His superior could help if he wanted, but the planewalker had made it clear that the cost would be too great.

Actions and consequences.

Yes, he thought.

He knew what Braxidane could do with his actions and consequences.

He looked for anything that might help. He rummaged in the debris, his strength coming back in bits as time passed. If he could find something that would get him back to Existence, he thought. Anything. But the city was a wasteland, and, with no store of life force Garrick didn't think he could make it to Existence on his own.

Will groaned.

The boy's eyes flickered open. They were dark and dilated.

Garrick tasted bile. Ettril was right about one thing.

This was his fault.

Sunathri. The Dorfort dead. Darien struggle at the helm of the Freeborn—they had all happened because he had been too afraid to take his role when he should have. And even now that he had agreed to take the Freeborn, he saw his reasons had been faulty. He had chosen to lead the order to spite Braxidane and the planewalkers, rather than from any real desire to help. Yes, doing so could ensure Adruin was free. But Garrick could not lie to himself. He had decided to take the Torean House purely so he could stand in the way of the planewalkers.

He cursed his short-sightedness.

It was all his fault.

And now Will lay here dying because Garrick had been too

protective to teach him enough magic to defend himself—even a simple bolt of energy might have been enough. "Garrick, sir," Will whispered, his teeth flashing white in the gloom. "I'm glad you're alive."

"I say the same for you. And you can still drop the *sir*, all right?"

Will swallowed with a bird-like movement. "I'm not sure ... for how much longer I'll make it, though."

"None of that, now."

"My belly hurts," Will said. "Inside."

Garrick's hunger twisted like a caged tiger as he felt the pain in Will. He needed to get the boy home or heal him, or face the fact that he was going to watch Will fade away before his very eyes.

His hunger moved like a shark inside him.

It gave him a thought that scared him.

He had grown comfortable channeling the wild energy from Braxidane's power through the gates of his standard sorcery, but he had never tried it the other way around, he had never used standard magestuff to drive his hunger. Could he use magestuff as he used life force? Ettril was dead now. The gates to the plane should be open. And if he was right about the essence of the two magics being the same, it might work.

He had no other ideas.

He set leverage points and opened his link. Energy poured over his gates. He thought back to the beginning, back to Arianna lying in the wooded creekbed as he poured magestuff into her. It hadn't worked then, but it was different now—his hunger was there inside him, and rather than merely dousing Will's wounds with pure wizardry he latched this stream of standard magic into his hunger, and then called on the hunger to rise. He drew more mage stuff into him, overloading his body, filling the repositories that fueled his Torean magic, and letting the rest pour through his body.

Braxidane's dark magic pulsed. He kept pushing. Heat rose. The hunger grew to a boil.

Finally, he dropped the gates that controlled the intake, dropped the gates that protected a mage from the rush of Talin's magestuff.

And it was like …

… drinking a lake in one, deep draught.

He breathed it in until he couldn't breathe further, then he kept drawing. Power engulfed him. Surrounded him. Scrubbed him from the inside. He was drowning in magestuff, and he felt the hunger inside become sated and fade as it belched upward into the flow of magestuff.

The hair rose on his neck. His skin tingled.

Energy flowed inside him, swirling, feeling cool and calm, and tasting so sweet and so similar to the life force that drove Braxidane's wild magic. More energy flowed. His body stopped aching, and his muscles smoothed. His ankle grew stronger.

Garrick turned to Will with magical fire flickering at his fingertips.

He wrapped his hands around the boy's head and sensed a cracked skull. Garrick pressed his mind into Will's body. He molded energy around the fracture, then moved to the boy's chest and innards. He poured energy, raw and free, into Will's injuries. Pancreas, spleen, liver, intestines. Every cell in Will's body was a separate entity that registered in Garrick's mind. He took his time, building them back instinctively, letting the life force have its way.

Finally, he pulled back and let his link free.

And Will's eyes flickered open.

FORTY-TWO

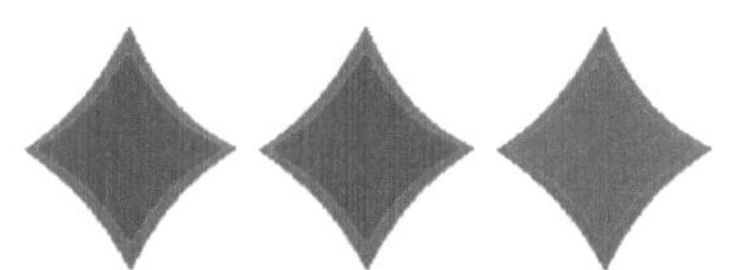

"You healed me," Will said.

Garrick gave a smirk and, in a slow movement, tousled the boy's hair. The gesture brought a sense of reality he desperately needed. He felt Will's heartbeat throb against his hunger. It was powerful and pure—the only thing other than himself that was alive on this plane.

"You didn't think I would leave you here, did you?"

Will didn't respond, but his thoughts colored his face. The boy had seen Garrick's dark magic work, and he knew Garrick had been drained of power just a few moments ago. So, when Garrick had reached toward him, Will had clearly expected to die.

"Come here," Garrick said, motioning the boy closer. "I'm going to get us home."

The boy came along, regardless of any fear he may have.

"This is going to be strange, but don't do anything surprising. Just relax, and I'll take care of you."

"Promise?"

Garrick gave a chuckle. "Yes, I promise. But I'm serious. I don't know if I can manage the process if you don't stay still, and I need to get it right or we could both be in for a lot of trouble."

Will nodded.

Garrick put his hand over the boy's shoulder, and Will wrapped an arm around Garrick's waist. He reached for his link. Magic flowed. He spoke a few words, and an orb formed around them both. Then Garrick grabbed a fold in the fabric of the plane and slipped through.

Will gasped at the essence of All of Existence.

Garrick enjoyed the sight of the boy's face as shifting hues of raw energy reflected off his cheekbones and glimmered in his eyes.

"What do you think?" he asked.

Will's mouth worked, but no words came out.

Garrick grinned and moved them through the flow.

He felt Braxidane's presence somewhere in the distance. If he paid attention he could feel planewalkers everywhere, though the concentration that effort took was immense. He could easily confront his superior if he wanted, but he didn't trust himself with Braxidane right now. He didn't understand what Braxidane was doing with him. And on top of that, he knew what Braxidane would say.

He had a bargain to uphold.

So instead, Garrick pictured Adruin and Dorfort, and he flowed Existence's energy into his spell work, letting power run through his body, picking at it, and giving himself time to recharge. He could do this again and again, couldn't he? When his hunger rose to its greatest heights, could he just step into Existence, and fill himself up? Did that mean that perhaps he would never need to kill again?

The idea made him laugh out loud.

Then it brought tears formed of a harsh mixture of joy and shame that burned in the fire of this place. Energy hissed, and the curve of their passage flowed.

"Are you all right, Garrick?" Will asked.

"Yes, Will. I am fine."

Garrick gritted his teeth, though, as his thoughts turned to Darien and the Freeborn.

This had been coming for a long time. He had known it somehow even before he had promised Braxidane to take control of the Torean House. But he thought about Darien and imagined his friend's reaction as he took that control.

In so many ways, taking command of the Freeborn would be the hardest thing he had ever done.

THE KORADICTINE PLAY

FORTY-THREE

The energy required to magic her way back to de'Mayer Island taxed Neuma greatly. She arrived numb from two nights without sleep, and in a mood that would scare off a planewalker's demon. But at least with Hirl-enat and Fil traveling to the Vapor Peaks, she had time to recover.

A little, anyway. Enough.

Badwall needed to be addressed—as did the entire western plain, for that matter—but that could wait until she had secured the island itself. Everyone with half a thought understood that the Koradictine order would survive as long as the island was held firm, and that meant ensuring the loyalty of the few wizards who remained.

She went to her basin to find it full of stagnant water.

"Hess?" she called, but there was no answer.

She stormed into the hallway.

While the Koradictine castle itself was an edifice that towered over de'Mayer point, the stronghold was a labyrinth of halls and rooms carved into the volcanic cliffs themselves. Befitting her age and experience rather than her power, her room was far from the interior. Hence the hallways were longer and darker than many others.

The path was familiar, though.

Her fatigue served to feed her anger as her stride picked up a steady rhythm. Her footsteps gave a staccato ring against the stone. The door to the kitchen was cracked open, allowing voices to leak out. The apprentices and adepts were eating together, or playing dice, or some other game of randomness that each would attempt to influence with the creative use of magestuff.

She remembered those times in her past, but was in no mood for games.

"Hess?" she said, stepping into the chamber.

Conversation came to an abrupt stop.

"Lady Neuma," Hess said, sliding his backside off the table where he had been holding court with, knowing him, some overblown tale of wonder.

"We were just on break, Lady Neuma," Hess said, bowing with submission.

"You've been on break for so long that you've forgotten to refresh my water?"

"We expected you back much later," he replied.

"Things change," she said. "It will go best for you if you anticipate that from now on."

"Yes, Lady. I'll get to the water right away."

Hess stepped past.

Neuma glanced at the remaining apprentices, thinking about Ettril and Hirl-enat. She was so close to the end game. So close.

"Things are changing around here for you, too," she said to the apprentices. "You had best prepare, too."

CHAPTER

FORTY-FOUR

Fil stopped scanning the woods to look at Hirl-enat.

The elder mage was riding on the bench seat beside him, his eyes closed, his head swaying with the motion of the wagon. He was younger than Ettril, but not as powerful. And his ability to see things for what they were was limited. He played things cautiously, never daring too much—unlike Neuma, whose ambition was worn like a garish streak of blush across her cheek.

He pulled his blanket up over his neck. How long would Hirl-enat last?

Though the weather had held reasonably fair, it had been a long trip—over a week's passage to the Vapor Peaks alone. It would be good to get this resolved so they could get home.

The party came to a halt, and Hirl-enat's eyes slid open.

Lectodinians, three of them, blocked the passage.

The lead figure was draped in the telltale blue of the order. A quick spell revealed several more mages scattered across the hillside. He had sensed Lectodinians often over the past two days, so this was not surprising. It was good, after all. It was why they had decided to travel so openly, hoping their transparency would draw this very opportunity to parley.

"What are you doing here?" the Lectodinian leader said.

Hirl-enat stood, brushed what wrinkles he could out of his robes, and stepped down.

Fil followed.

"We wish to speak to your Lord Superior," Hirl-enat said.

"I am sure he is occupied."

"I believe he will be unoccupied when you tell him we are interested in discussing a merger."

The mage gave a perceptible pause.

"Go ahead and contact him," Hirl-enat said. "We will wait."

Fil observed everything, storing it away.

He noticed how Hirl-enat's eyes danced with humor at the Lectodinian's reaction to the idea the Koradictines might surrender, and he noted the way the Lectodinian's hands shook with more than the cold of winter as he entered his communication spell.

Fil was impressed with Hirl-enat's composure. His was the key role in this charade. He had to sell the decoy, had to be believed when he promised Koradictine service to the Lectodinian agenda. Neuma's plan was a good one if Hirl-enat could do this part. Without a quiet span over the winter months, the Koradictine order may well be destroyed, so it was imperative his tone be convincing. So far, he had played the part to perfection.

"Lord Esta will see you," the mage finally replied. "We will escort you from this point."

Hirl-enat tipped his head. "Excellent."

THEY WERE LED into the Lectodinian stronghold through a set of passages cut into the cold, sheer cliffs of the Vapor Peaks. The passes reminded Fil of those his own order had dug into the volcanic realms of de'Mayer Island and the Canyons of Badwall. As they progressed, Fil felt the complex weave of spellwork behind the Lectodinian security systems. From the occasional glances he received from Hirl-enat he was certain the elder felt them also.

That was good.

They didn't need anything to go awry here, and if Hirl-enat sensed the spell-cover, perhaps he would be even more cautious.

The Lectodinians brought them to a social chamber that was small and blessedly warm thanks to a fire that burned brightly from a hearth built into one wall.

Fil and Hirl-enat were seated. A ring of Lectodinian wizards stood around the perimeter, waiting. The span was long enough that Fil considered the idea that perhaps they had been brought to an ambush chamber. Then sounds of disturbance came from the hallways, and Zutrian Esta, High Superior of the Lectodinian order, entered.

The Lord said nothing, merely paused, took them in, and then took the padded chair beside the fire. Once he sat, a pair of the wait staff brought a small table of simple carpentry and placed it between Zutrian and the Koradictines, another brought goblets of warmed wine. Zutrian took a goblet, and still without speaking motioned Hirl-enat and Fil to help themselves.

Fil was tired, and he was hungry, and, despite the warmth of the room—or perhaps because of it—he was feeling the effects of the winter roads. It was all he could do to stop himself from bolting down the wine.

"I don't see the value," Zutrian finally said.

"You don't see the value in joining our two great orders?"

"The Koradictines ceased to be a great order when Garrick cut your ranks at God's Tower, and what he wasn't able to finish, internal squabbling and civil unrest in the western plane has managed to complete for him."

"It is true we are weakened," Hirl-enat said with more calm than Fil had expected. "But the Koradictine order has roots that run deep.

We are far from defenseless, and far from powerless. If you will not bond with us, we can cause you great pain."

"Roots that run deep," Zutrian mused. "Yes. Like weeds, you are."

"Aptly described," Hirl-enat replied. "Much, I would guess, as the Lectodinians would be had Garrick driven down the eastern face of God's Tower on that fateful day rather than the westward face."

Zutrian's smile was more of a smirk.

Fil was growing more impressed over time. There was more to Hirl-enat than he had expected.

"You know as well as I do, Lord Esta, that this is the one difference between our positions—the random fact that Garrick encountered *our* lines rather than yours is the only reason our orders find themselves in such different states. We are not weaker than you due to any inherent flaw in our order. We are weaker than you because Garrick surprised us and not you. And you know as well as we do that as long as the god-touched still draws breath, you could be next."

Hirl-enat paused.

"No," he said, continuing. "You *will* be next."

The Lectodinian smiled and sipped from his goblet.

"And the dredges of the Koradictine order can help me?"

"We can still sting," Hirl-enat said. "And we have one advantage that the Lectodinians cannot have."

"Which would be?"

"Garrick thinks we are dead."

This comment brought a slow smile to Zutrian's face. "Yes," he said. "I can see how that could be used to an advantage."

This was the point where Fil knew they had won.

THEY FINISHED the negotiation two days later. They had agreed to work with Zutrian, agreed to meet regularly, and agreed to focus their efforts on shadowing Dorfort to report happenings around Garrick and the Torean Freeborn. They would hinder them at all points, of course, assuming Garrick returned to the city, anyway.

The Lectodinians would spread themselves eastward first—away from the Koradictine stronghold, while the Koradictines regained what hold they could in the west.

And in the springtime, when travel was better, they would join under one banner. Zutrian would accept the helm of this new, consolidated order of mages. Hirl-enat, Fil, and Neuma would all receive key roles in the new governance, and the group as a whole would use the Koradictine learning to finish the one task that everyone agreed needed to be undertaken: the killing of Garrick.

"That was well-played," Fil told Hirl-enat after the council had disbanded. "You've bought us an entire winter without Lectodinian disruption."

"We'll need it," Hirl-enat said, staring ahead.

Fil sat back. They were rested and ready. Tomorrow they would begin the trip back to de'Mayer Island. He sensed both of them were thinking the same thing—both wondering what surprises Neuma had for them when they returned.

CHANGING OF THE
GUARD

FORTY-FIVE

Garrick brought them straight to Dorfort.

Knowing it was the most likely place to find Darien, Garrick walked from the courtyard, into the government center, and toward his friend's chamber. Though the winter chill kept the hallway cold, the excess energy he had carried back from Existence kept him warm and vigorous.

There would be rumors about him, he knew.

One does not disappear as he had without rumors. And one does not physically threaten the ruler of a land without repercussions.

And if those actions didn't cause a big enough stir, his actual appearance now certainly would. His wounds had been healed while he waded through Existence, but sweat and blood had etched a spider web of trails across his face. His shirt and breeches were tattered and scorched from demon touch and from Ettril's wizardry. A diagonal slice in his pant leg exposed the skin of his thigh.

Those in the courtyard had backed away with eyes wide as he strode through their midst, his breath billowing in the winter cold and his boots crunching over layers of snow. The government center's yard smelled the same as he remembered, brown dirt with a coating of the briny fresh air of Blue Lake. Fires burned from pits with greasy black smoke, and the aroma of yeasty rye came from ovens in the back.

He passed these onlookers, unheeding of their stares.

Will followed behind.

A guard stepped forward to block his way. It was a sergeant, a man named Harol—one of Darien's many friends in the city's service. He wore the leathered plate of Dorfort's guard under layers of cloth and fur. The city's red and yellow insignia blazed on his shield. His eyes were brown marbles that gazed directly at Garrick, seemingly unfazed by his aura of power.

"Where is Darien?" Garrick asked.

Harol's eyes hardened further. "Not where he should be."

Garrick paused. "What's wrong?"

"The captain is in the chamber hall with the gaggle of mages that wear your colors."

"Isn't that to be expected?" said Will.

"Not when he should be minding funeral arrangements."

Garrick's heart dropped. "Commander J'ravi?"

Harol stared at him. "He passed last eve."

"Dour news," Garrick said.

"Yes, it is. But today the Toreans have something important going on, so Lord Darien is too preoccupied to attend to his father's arrangements. I stand guard over the funeral room until he can be available."

Garrick nodded. "I am sorry to hear this."

The guard gave a sorrowful sigh, and the muscles across his forehead relaxed. Despite appearances, he had been afraid of what Garrick might do.

"What issue is taking Darien away?"

"No offense intended, Lord, but I never did understand wizards even a hair's width, and I don't care to start now."

Garrick turned to Will, who was shivering in the cold.

"Stay with the sergeant. I need to see what I can do with the Freeborn."

"Yes, Master Garrick."

"Harol, can you get the boy something warmer to wear?"

"Aye, Lord. I'll see to it."

"Thank you."

Garrick strode again through the hallway, and again toward the government center's meeting chamber.

What could be so important as to draw Darien from his father's side? He couldn't imagine anything beyond the total destruction of the city. These thoughts darkened his mood as he walked, his boots clicking off time. Loud voices came from behind the pair of closed, double doors that led to the meeting hall.

Garrick pressed the bronze latch and pulled the door open, giving himself free passage into the midst of a raging argument.

FORTY-SIX

A wave of heat and angry voices rolled through the hall. Reynard stood at the dais, shaking a finger at Darien like a mother giving her child a warning. His face was red as a beet.

The Freeborn were positioned in disarray throughout the chamber—some standing, some yelling with voices now going hoarse, some seated on pallet benches arguing with their neighbors, and some loitering in the corners with silent, but dour expressions.

The chamber's high ceilings gave the room a rounded echo—making it exceptional for speeches, debates, music, and theatre. But now those ceilings molded the arguments into a single, unintelligible roar that hit like a hammer.

Darien was the first to notice Garrick's presence.

He stood next to Reynard, leaning forward with both hands on the table and looking over his constituency with a black-eyed gaze. His shoulders were hunched, and his gold-threaded cape draped him as if he wished he could hide behind it.

His expression at seeing Garrick was a mixture of relief and anger. He said nothing, but he stood up taller and squared his shoulders.

Garrick strode toward the front of the chamber.

One by one, voices quieted as he drew nearer to the dais until there was only a single voice remaining—that of Reynard.

"If you think you can run over this order—" he spoke to Darien before turning to see the distraction. His voice froze and his pointed finger hung in mid-shake.

Garrick stood before the two of them, glancing first at Reynard, then at Darien.

A sense of detachment came over him.

He turned, taking in the room. Heat rose to his cheeks, and he felt the presence of each mage around the room.

"What is this argument about?" he asked.

Darien smoothed his hands down his hips. "It's a long tale."

"Give me the short version."

Reynard began. "Our superior—"

Garrick stifled him.

Darien's inability to hold a steady gaze told Garrick just how nervous he was.

"I've developed a policy designed to save lives," Darien said. "But the rest of the order does not agree with it."

Garrick turned to Reynard.

"It is a senseless policy that will do nothing but steal energy from mages that would be better used elsewhere. It's *another* case of a man with no common sense trying to force his opinion—"

Garrick held up his hand again.

"I see," he said. "I can't believe you called a meeting about such a trivial procedure when our leader is grieving for his father."

The order hung on his silence.

There was more to this than he first thought. Garrick sensed that now. Something else was happening here, something deeper. Garrick saw it in Darien's face. "You," he said, pointing to Amanda, a young woman whom Sunathri had personally recruited.

All eyes turned to her.

She was blonde and tiny, perhaps a handful of years older than Will. Her bones were thin and her face bird-like. Garrick remembered how everyone had thought Amanda would be weak in the battle at God's Tower, how they thought casting sorcerous energy for so long would overwhelm her. But Amanda, the daughter of a noblewoman in Passidian, had surprised them all. Her gift was strong, and her magic had saved lives. More important to the moment, Garrick had come to see her as one who would speak her mind clearly and without adornment.

She cleared her throat.

"Darien called the session, Lord."

His brows furrowed.

"While searching for the boy, Superior J'ravi's party was overrun in the night. He had set a sentry, though. It wasn't his fault."

She was going to be a good leader, Garrick thought.

He listened further as Amanda related pertinent details about the incident.

"Thank you Amanda," Garrick said when she was finished.

He understood now. He saw Darien's frustration.

On the evening his father passed, Darien had been away, and he had lost his men. Darien, a man who lived in constant competition with his brother—a brother who had believed in the collective good so boldly that he had died for it—had come up short again. And, Garrick saw how the Freeborn—an order founded on Sunathri's principles of equal value and personal liberty—would fight Darien's controls with the very root of their existence.

He didn't want this to happen now. His friend was downtrodden and needed support from Garrick—but the people here needed him to be bold and decisive. In the end, drawing it out would just be cruel.

"Darien saved this order. I'm sure most of you remember how it felt to see him at the helm those months ago, knowing that we needed him to take this responsibility merely so the Freeborn could exist."

Reynard spoke again. "That was before—"

"And perhaps some of you will remember another time. Sunathri's time. I know I do. I remember her offering me a position. It was more than an offer, of course. It was a plea. She believed in me more than I believed in myself, and she put herself on display in front of all of you by rescuing me, then offering me leadership of the order she, herself, had created. Think of the sacrifice that took. Think of the passion."

Heads nodded.

"Most of you know that story," Garrick said. "I'm sure it was told over campfires for months afterward. But only a few know that when I turned her down, Sunathri did something important. Something that defines the vision she had in creating this House to begin with. Something we all need to remember right now."

Garrick moved to stand before Amanda. The silence that filled the chamber was now reverential.

"Do you know what she did?" he asked her.

Amanda shook her head.

"She sat beside me."

Garrick smiled and turned to the rest of the mages.

"I remember the wind picking through Sunathri's hair. The way the overcast sky had darkened her skin. I remember the heat of her passion for this order, the intense stare that seemed so bold it could burn you if you dared to let it into your soul."

He looked across the room and saw smiles on several faces.

"She told me I was free to go, but that she would not be the first to leave. She said she had founded this order so that every human being on this plane—or any other plane, for that matter—would be free to do what they wanted to do, free to be what they wanted to be. She said she would sit beside me regardless of my choice, that while I may leave the Freeborn, the Freeborn would never leave me."

A man cleared his throat in the back of the room.

Garrick motioned toward Darien.

"Darien J'ravi—son of Dorfort's commander, and a hero of the magewar—has given much to this order. He has led our armies to victory on the fields and has kept us together these past months while we sorted out who we are. He has done us a remarkable service."

Garrick glanced at Reynard.

"For that, we are *all* in his debt."

Then he turned directly to Darien. His friend's gaze trembled. To lose the order now would crush Darien, but there was no other course.

"But I believe that I understand my purpose, now. I believe that for the first time, I understand Sunathri's vision, and hence I understand exactly what I am called on to do. It is time, my friend," he said to Darien. "Time that I step forward to take the role Sunathri asked me to take so long ago, and it is time for you to tend to your father."

Darien nodded, resigned now, his eyes growing cold, and his lips set. "Then that is how it will be," Darien said. "I hand whatever title I have to Garrick. May he find more success than I have."

An awkward silence followed.

Finally, a mage put his hands together in a single clap, then another, and another. One by one, the mages of the order joined and the sound grew to a deafening crescendo. The mages came forward, then, cheering and clapping.

Garrick stepped into the crowd, amid the sound of voices that were once again gathered into a single force. Hands reached out to touch his arm, or pat him on the back.

"Hail Darien," Garrick called over the voices.

The hallway erupted in another round of cheering. "Hail Darien! Hail Garrick!"

But when Garrick turned to include his friend, the seat behind the table was empty.

Darien J'ravi, deposed leader of the Freeborn House of mages, had left the chamber.

EPILOGUE

Neuma would have preferred to meet Hirl-enat somewhere less personal, but he and Fil had returned to de'Mayer Island yesterday, and it was important she get this done now. So she stepped into the elder mage's chamber.

Hirl-enat looked up from his papers, fountain quill in hand.

"What do you want?" he said.

"I wanted to welcome you home and congratulate you on your success." She extended her hand.

Hirl-enat relaxed as he reached to take it.

Sorcerous energy from the plane of magic poured into Neuma's mind. She twisted it, letting the power dance across her fingers, its aura a bluish green as it crossed over gates she had already prepared.

Hirl-enat's defense was too late.

Neuma's forked charge filled the chamber—a single blast of electricity that shook the area's walls. Hirl-enat's shield imploded with its own force.

The elder mage died before he knew what had happened.

Silence and the odor of roasted flesh settled over the room.

Neuma stooped to examine Hirl-enat's body. It was charred and crisped. She could barely contain her smile. Her stomach did flip-flops. The expression on the old man's face had been perfect.

I knew it, that expression had said. *I knew you were a traitor!*

Better a conniver, she thought, than a fool.

She rose and checked her link again, searching once more for a connection to Ettril, but there was no response. After such a long absence, the Koradictine high superior was almost certainly now dead. And she had personally taken out Quin Sar and Hirl-enat.

Neuma's grin spread across her face, and she sighed with contentment.

It could not have worked out any better.

There was much to do, though, and little time for celebration. The Lectodinians had damaged the order, but she had something new in her favor now. She had followed Ettril's link to the god-planes of All Existence. She had felt Hezarin's raw anger and sensed how far the planewalker would be willing to go for her vengeance.

Hezarin had lost her mage.

But she would help *Neuma* now because *Neuma* could help Hezarin. The challenge would be arriving at a plan that dealt with both the Lectodinians and Garrick at the same time.

Tricky, but achievable.

She straightened her robe, then left to take control of her order.

This is the end of *Rogue Mage*. I greatly value feedback. If you have enjoyed this story so far, please consider returning to your favorite booksellers and leaving a review.

The story of Garrick, Darien, and the struggle between the orders continues in *Champion Mage,* available as another tenth-anniversary edition of *Saga of the God-Touched Mage.*

The Saga of the God-Touched Mage
(10th Anniversary Edition)
includes

Apprentice Mage
Rogue Mage
Champion Mage
God Mage

Acknowledgments

The universe of Adruin and All of Existence has many people to thank for its existence, not the least of which are Tim Brown, Mike Cox, Ken and Jackie Peters, and my wife, Lisa.

I need to single out a few others for their efforts beyond all the rest.

My friend, collaborator, and pre-reader John Bodin's help was—as always—superlative. I want to thank my daughter, Brigid, for stepping into the fray when I needed her. And I want to give thanks to both my original cover artist, Rachel Carpenter, who was great fun to work with and who did a fantastic job bringing Garrick to life, and to Lisa Silverthorne who blew my mind with her great work on this 10th Anniversary edition.

Mostly, though, I have to thank Lisa for everything she's done for me. *Saga of the God-Touched Mage* has gone through more twists and turns than I could ever have predicted when the idea first hit, and she's been with me through every step. (Don't worry, honey. It's really done. Really, I mean it. It's done. You don't have to read it for the 111th time!).

ABOUT RON COLLINS

Ron Collins is a bestselling Science Fiction and Dark Fantasy author who writes across the spectrum of speculative fiction.

Both his science fiction series, *Stealing the Sun*, and his fantasy series, *Saga of the God-Touched Mage*, have been bestsellers. His short fiction has received a Writers of the Future prize. He has published numerous short stories in venues such as *Analog, Asimov's, Pulphouse*, and the *Fiction River* original anthology project. His short stories have been listed on the preliminary ballot for SFWA's Nebula Award, and "The White Game" was nominated for the Short Mystery Fiction Society's Derringer Award.

His latest books are *Home Run Enchanted, Curveball Cursed*, and *Outfield Magicked*, which comprise the Fairies and Fastballs series, written with his daughter.

NEWSLETTER & CONTACT

Discover other work by Ron Collins at:
https://www.typosphere.com

Join Ron's Reader List, and get free books!:
https://typosphere.com/newsletter